Dungeon Crawl

The Twenty-Sided Sorceress: Book Eight

Annie Bellet

Cover designed by Ravven (www.ravven.com)
Formatting by Polgarus Studio (www.polgarusstudio.com)
First edition, 2017

If you want to be notified when Annie Bellet's next novel is released and get free stories and occasional other goodies, please sign up for her mailing list by going to: http://tinyurl.com/anniebellet Your email address will never be shared and you can unsubscribe at any time.

Dedicated to the best DnD group: Andrew, Hank, Vandy, Ursula, Brian, and Jeremy.

It looks good to me, guys!

Pwned Comics and Games had its grand opening party on a balmy day at the end of August. The finishing touches weren't on my shop yet, a few odds and ends left to do like painting the baseboards in the new office area I'd created behind the now-built-in counters and cases. But it was home, renewed.

Home with better lighting, a kick-ass wireless network, surround sound, and bamboo flooring. Between what Ciaran and Brie had kicked in and the money I'd practically throttled out of my insurance company from the fire, we'd managed to build a suite of shops on the block that would do Wylde, Idaho proud. I'd heard from a couple of other shops on the blocks around us that they were planning to copy the dark purple awnings and faux-stone facing.

Most of a year gone since the town had come under siege by my evil ex. Sometimes it felt like a lifetime ago. Sometimes like only a minute. Trauma is like that, I guess. The town rebounded okay, and so had I.

Most days.

This was one of the good days. The shop was open for business, lots of people, human and shifter alike, dropped in. Ciaran had re-opened his shop a few weeks prior, but with all my custom lighting I'd had to wait a little before my part was ready. Plus I'd sunk more time into the new digs upstairs, because living in a trailer with a giant tiger wasn't the most exciting thing in the world. Turns out Alek and I like a little space.

Brie's bakery had been operating out of a temporary location, but all was ready for her own opening in two days. She had proper stone counters and ovens that had made the gold-loving Leprechaun blink when he saw the receipts.

The sun had dropped behind the building and only the hum of the air conditioner broke the quiet as I shut down the computer at the counter. Closing time. After locking the front door, I threaded my way through the racks of comics toward the steps leading up. That new home smell still clung to the space. Fresh paint fumes lingered in the air. I was going to have to spill some Mountain Dew on my new, pristine, and environmentally friendly floors.

I shook my head at myself. Fat chance I could bring myself to do that. The second story was all gaming rooms now, including a dedicated LAN space. Which is where the true opening party was taking place, with the twins, Ezee and Levi, already waiting for me. It was a new season of Diablo III and my Demon Hunter wasn't going to level herself.

"I ordered pizza," said the love my life in his growly Russian accent. Alek was sitting on the top step but he stood up as I climbed toward him.

"You know how to win our hearts," I said, poking him in his ridiculously hard belly.

"You will game all night and forget to eat," Alek said, his ice-blue eyes narrowing. The light at the top of the steps turned his white-blond hair into a golden halo.

"It's the gamer diet," I said, leaning into him. "How else will we keep our perfect physiques?"

"Kettlebells?" Alek said.

His voice rumbled his chest and I sighed, breathing

deep of his sweet and spice scent. He had a way of making everything okay. He'd proven himself pretty handy with electrical wiring and tile grouting, too.

"Not today, torturer. Tonight, we game!" He had me doing all kinds of crazy exercises and while I saw the point after wishing countless times in the last couple years that I was in better shape, there was only so much compromise a girl could make. Diablo before bros, right? "Sure you don't want to join us?"

"I will wait for pizza," he said. I felt his muscles ripple under his teeshirt as he shook his head.

"Offer is always open." I pulled away from him and squeezed past him up to the landing. Second door on the right, straight on till morning.

The LAN room had six custom-built gaming computers arrayed on a half-circle table. Because this was my joint, I'd built them to my own specs, putting in the chairs I liked best, using the mice and keyboards I favored. Nobody had complained, but given how good I was with a fireball and how half the town, the non-human half anyway, knows it, I figured nobody would dare. At the moment the table faced away from the door, because I wanted people to be able to come in and check out the action, but I was thinking about switching it. Sitting with my back to a door made me twitchy these days. Just another thing I'd be testing out tonight.

The Chapowitz twins, Ezee and Levi, were already upstairs, having escaped to make sure everything was loaded and the profiles all set up before we commenced the true breaking in of our new gamer haven. Levi had his Mohawk pulled into a tight knot on his head, I assumed to keep it off his neck in the heat, and was already in the loading screen, clearly impatient to get started. Ezee had shed his custom suit in favor of a more summer-friendly XKCD teeshirt that said "Science. It works, bitches" on it and khaki shorts, and was leaning back in his chair, sipping a cold Dr. Pepper.

"Everything set?" I asked Ezee as I slid into my chair. "I see you found the soda." I could tell his can was fresh out of the mini-fridge from the condensation beading around his fingers and threatening to drip onto my brand new floors. Guess things couldn't and wouldn't stay pristine forever.

"Ready when you are. Let's do this." Ezee saluted me with the soda.

"First one to die has to eat a ghost pepper," Levi said. We were playing hardcore mode, of course, which meant that any death was permanent and if you died you had to start a new character.

"That's between you two. I ain't part of that bet, nope. Leave me out of it." I tugged my braid over my shoulder and then cracked my knuckles. Time to click click click some monsters into oblivion and save the world.

Unlike saving the world for realsies, this was low stress, low impact. Best part about video games was even though we were playing hardcore mode, none of the deaths would really be forever.

None of us brought up the missing fourth party member. None of us had to. There was a Harper-sized hole in everything we did, but until she was ready to get back in touch, until she was ready to come home… well. There wasn't much to be done now but eat, sleep, game, repeat.

We were leveling by running bounties in Act One and managing not to totally wipe out when I heard Alek coming up the steps. I'd wondered what was taking pizza so long. If this slaughter kept up we'd be taking a death break in a minute anyway.

"Stop spamming your AOE like that, Levi." Frustration made Ezee's voice crack.

"Zomg, lag," I said. The game wasn't without its flaws and these were brand new untested computer rigs, after all.

"I'm doing damage!" Levi retorted.

"Yeah, damage to our video cards."

"It's nice to see that some things never change," a woman's voice said from where the door was behind me.

I let my Demon Hunter perish as I spun around. Harper stood in the doorway with a lopsided grin, her green eyes betraying her uncertainty as she hesitated.

"Furball!" I practically levitated across the space to hug her. At the last second I paused, realizing she might not want to be mobbed by a sweating, manic woman she hadn't seen in almost a year.

"Hey you," she said, stepping into me, reaching across the distance. She was just as sweaty and neither of us cared as I danced her around in a tiny circle.

Ezee and Levi joined in, all of us talking at once.

"We saw your crazy game at the qualifier."

"I missed you so freaking much."

"Did you come straight in from the airport?"

"I just came from the airport. Pizza is here, Alek said he'll put it in the tabletop room."

"Guys," I said as I pushed apart the hug mob. "Give her a minute."

"Sure, yeah."

"We're dead anyway. Ezee died first. Ghost pepper before or after pizza?"

"Jade died first, so it doesn't count."

"Wait, who is eating a ghost pepper?" Harper looked around as Ezee pointed at me and Levi pointed at Ezee.

"Not happening," I said.

"Pizza," Alek said over Harper's head as he materialized in the doorway. "Ghost free."

"You got a place to stay?" Ezee asked, then looked like he wanted to kick himself for reminding Harper that her home had been destroyed.

She smiled at him as though to say, hey, it's okay, and shook her head. "I'll figure it out."

"We have a guest room now," I said. "You are welcome as long as you want."

"A guest room? Wow, you are like a real adult," Harper said. "I left my bag downstairs."

"We'll have to give you a tour of the new shop," Levi said. "Jade made it awesomer."

"I missed a lot," Harper said, looking around.

"Not that much. Been pretty quiet," I said. "Other than the daily construction, that wasn't quiet, obviously." I wanted to kick myself for the awkwardness that had crept over me.

"And that whole thing with Jade and Bigfoot," Levi added, making me want to kick him.

"Bigfoot? What?" Harper looked at me.

Universe save me. I wasn't going into that story standing here half inside the LAN room. Nope.

"You both go eat pizza, I'll run Harper up to the apartment and let her put stuff down, then we can do the catching-up thing." I shooed everyone into the hall.

At the bottom of the stairs, Harper hesitated again as she lifted her bag up and turned back to me.

"You sure it's okay if I stay with you?" she asked.

"Harper," I said, taking her shoulders in my hands and tugging her closer. She seemed thinner under my fingers, the bones of her shoulders more pronounced. "You are family. I told you that you'd always have a spot at the table. That hasn't changed. That'll never change."

Her eyes looked less haunted than they had when she'd left on that wintry night months ago, but her face was more lined than it had been and shadows still lurked within the green depths of her irises. She'd lost more than most of us to Samir's evil plans. We were kin now in that way, too. Samir had cost both of us our families and our homes.

"I'm sorry I didn't respond to your emails," she said softly. "I had to figure shit out."

"Did you?"

"Kinda. I learned that shit happens. I guess I could have bought a bumper sticker instead, but eh. Gotta do it the hard way, right?" She grinned and it looked almost feral in the dim light from the stairs.

"I tried to run," she added, "But I figured out that if you're running from something, it just follows you."

I smiled back at her, not saying that I could have told her that. I'd learned about running away from trouble the hard way. So many had paid for my mistakes, including my best friend.

Harper had changed, I imagined, in ways that none of us understood yet. But it didn't matter. What I'd said stood. She was family and she was home. I pulled her into another hug and her arms came around me, squeezing with almost painful strength.

"Welcome home, furball," I murmured.

The dream is always the same. I am never alone, Wolf walks beside me, always growling low as though some threat will spring out. The house I walk through is one my waking self has never seen, but my dream-self knows it in that oddly strange-but-familiar way dream places are.

Samir is always there as well. Lurking. Sometimes just a flash of golden eyes that disappear through a doorway before I can catch his gaze. Sometimes he's a dark figure in a long hallway, silhouetted against the dim light from a distant room. Always gone before I can reach him. He never speaks.

Until tonight.

"Not the calm, but the eye," he whispers, his voice familiar as it crawls under my skin and inside my head. "The center cannot hold."

I woke up sweating, clutching my twenty-sided die talisman in both hands, a sob dying in my throat. Beside me, Alek woke also, his body tense, alert to whatever had brought me sitting bolt upright.

"Just a dream," I said. I felt around in the near dark until my hand closed on the hilt of Alpha and Omega, the magical knife the vampire known as the Archivist had given me when I was fighting Samir.

Alek turned on the lamp on his side of the bed. One of the upsides of having my old place burn down was the new apartment was much larger. Large enough to have a guest room, and a bedroom that could fit a king-size bed. That's important when your boyfriend is a six and a half foot tiger shifter.

"Thanks," I said, knowing Alek didn't need the light and had done that for my benefit.

The knife could destroy anything, alive or not. Except, apparently, sorcerers. It had reduced Samir down to a hard little gem, like a single drop of blood trapped inside a diamond or ruby. I didn't know if Samir could regenerate from that, but he technically wasn't dead until another sorcerer, such as myself, swallowed that final drop of heart's blood and took his memories and power.

Not something I was ready to do for a million reasons. The biggest being that it would apparently break one of the seals holding back ancient magics and creatures from the world and bring about a magical apocalypse.

Hence the dagger ritual I performed every morning. Or, like now, whenever I awoke freaking out about a damn dream.

I carefully unsheathed the dagger and pressed it against the tiny, glinting red gem that was set in my talisman right where the one would be on the die. Critical fail was a pretty accurate storage place for Samir, on so very many levels. The gem flickered with dim red light and then went dark and quiet again.

Not today, asshole.

"The dream again?" Alek rubbed my thigh through the thin sheet, his ice-blue eyes pale and concerned in the wan light from the little bedside lamp.

Nodding, I re-sheathed the dagger and put it back on the nightstand. I looked over at the clock. Just past five in the morning.

"Guess I might as well go make some breakfast," I said. I wasn't getting back to sleep. "Maybe I'll go crazy since Harper is back and make bacon and waffles."

Alek pulled me into his warm arms and nuzzled my hair. "I have another suggestion."

His hands slipped under my teeshirt and made it clear what his suggestion entailed. Sometimes Alek's perceptiveness and uncanny ability to read body language was annoying as hell. Sometimes there were definite benefits to having a lover and partner to whom nonverbal communication was totally normal.

"The gentleman wins," I said, turning my head to kiss him. The nebulous foreboding of the dream faded away as Alek reminded me of what mattered. Love. Family. And a really big bed.

"Since nobody wanted to live in Peggy's house after what happened, the town bought it. They're going to tear it down and make a memorial park, but now nobody can agree in the town meetings about who to memorialize and how, so it's just sitting condemned." I poured myself another mug of tea and sat back down at the table. "And that's all the Wylde news that's fit to print, I guess."

We'd been trying to make conversation but it felt like every topic at breakfast was a reminder of what had changed, what had been lost. Peggy, our former librarian and a witch who had been spying for Samir before she was killed by him last winter, wasn't exactly a safe topic, but it was pretty much the only news going on in town right now.

"I like the tile you picked for the bathroom," Harper said around a mouthful of bacon.

"Thanks," I said. "I didn't even know you could get custom tile prints. I thought the D&D dice thing might be too repetitive, but it seems to work." The tiles with their little polyhedral prints made me happy every time I went in there. Alek had shrugged and given no opinion on how we decorated the new place beyond "not too much pink, yes?" so I got to make all the decisions.

I'd gone almost full nerd, I admit. The carpet in both bedrooms had a repeating sword pattern. The bathroom tile was printed with dice. The bathmats were Pokemon themed, since Pokemon cards and the like had helped pay for this place, after all. A friendly dragon dispensed toilet paper, kind of as a reminder that I might be a dragon, but I shouldn't get all full of myself, or something to that effect. It amused me anyway. The kitchen was more tasteful with its black stone counters and stainless steel tile backsplash. I couldn't resist hanging dragon and white tiger printed curtains I'd found online. Those had gotten a smile out of Alek when he helped me hang them.

Alek stood up from the table. "I should get to work," he said, bending down to kiss the top of my head.

"Work?" Harper asked him.

I realized we hadn't even gotten to that yet as we talked over breakfast.

"He's helping Sheriff Lee as a consultant," I said.

"Even the human police find someone who can tell when someone is lying very helpful," Alek added.

"They believe you?" Harper raised her eyebrows skeptically.

"I have proved it over and over," Alek said as he put his breakfast dishes into the dishwasher. "Human cops watch a lot of TV. They believe I read micro-expression. Is good enough. I am good at interrogations and going with Rachel gives her safety in numbers."

"So you're on the brute squad?" Harper said with a grin.

"I am the brute squad," Alek said with a straight face. His ice-blue eyes were full of amusement and pleasure at recognizing the Princess Bride reference and being able to complete the quote.

"I see you've been getting an education while I was gone," Harper said.

"Yes. I am very smart now," Alek said, his lips twitching which ruined his stoic façade.

"I'll give you a tour of the shop after I clean up from breakfast," I told Harper as Alek went to put his boots on.

"So many changes," she said very softly.

"So much the same," I said.

Harper stayed with us for less than a week. She ran into Vivian, the town vet and a wolf shifter, while having coffee at Brie's bakery, and found out that the vet desperately needed someone part time to help answer the phone, keep an eye on sick animals, and help with appointments. Harper didn't need the job, I didn't think, but she took it to help out. She admitted to me she also took it in part so she could feel like she belonged here again. Hearing that about broke my heart, but I kept it to myself.

Harper found a studio unit to rent in a converted house on the University side of town and moved in there the same day she started working for Vivian.

First game night with her back could have been awkward, too, but somehow it wasn't. I wove her character back into the ongoing story with ease, as though she'd never been gone. It was a relief to have her, though she still didn't open up about what had happened while she was away beyond answering Levi's question about if she knew any of the people who got killed at those gaming conventions with a curt "yeah, I did," said in a tone that warned off any and all questions.

She'd tell me when she was ready, I hoped. I wasn't going to push her. I didn't feel like I had the right.

I was super relieved when after another week, she showed up on a day she wasn't helping Vivian, flopped into one of the two overstuffed chairs I had put near the comics, pulled out her laptop and asked for the WiFi password. Looking around the shop as I listened to Harper swearing at her computer screen, I realized that *now* it felt like home again. Funny how sometimes you don't notice exactly what is missing until it returns.

I had a new employee, a college student recommended by Ezee, to watch the counter and deal with anyone while I ate lunch or did admin work or whatever couldn't get done while I had to mind the front. Her name was Lara just like the video game character but that's where the similarities stopped. Employee Lara was short, stocky, and black, and if she was a British millionaire, she was definitely good at hiding it. She was a history student with a minor in Spanish up at Juniper College but she'd grown up in Seattle.

Oh, and she was another coyote shifter, like Ezee. I had a suspicion that was a reason he'd recommended her, but she turned out to be a nerd as well, though not into video games as much as comics, especially the

Marvel and Image company lines. I didn't care if she did her homework or caught up on comics while keeping an eye on the place and helping me keep the gaming areas clean, so we'd reached a good quiet equilibrium within a week of her working for me. Classes had just officially started, but she'd worked her schedule so she could cover a break for me in the middle of the day and be here in the afternoons when we were likely to actually see customers in my sleepy little town.

Sometimes when it was a slow day, which was most days in Wylde, Alek would leave Sheriff Lee to do paperwork and return phone calls, and bring me lunch. Today's lunch was take-out from the Chinese place. It was still warm, as it often was when the kids were returning to school, sort of a sunny fuck you to all the students who now had to be stuck inside, so we ate out in the back of the store.

"For you." Alek put a container of what smelled like fried rice on the counter and Lara beamed up at him.

"Charming my staff," I muttered as we walked out to the back where I had put in a little patio complete with a cover.

Alek put the bag of food down on the picnic table

I'd had made custom to fit the space and grinned at me.

"I like that you have time free," Alek said. "Keeping Lara happy is good for me."

I laughed and flopped onto the bench across from him. I couldn't argue with that. With Harper back, the store fully open, and students back at the college so I had regular business again, life felt almost normal.

Tires squealed as a car took the turn into my back parking lot a little too quickly and I had a protection shield half up before it halted. Magic hummed in my blood, burning to be free. I hadn't had much use for it besides in training these last months.

The car was a small blue Honda and I saw Levi's mohawked, pierced visage in the driver's seat as it jerked to a stop just in front of where we were. I let the spell go as Alek re-holstered the gun he'd drawn without me even noticing. My mate continued standing and I rose to go stand by him. If Levi was driving like that, something was wrong.

"Is Junebug okay?" I asked, referring to Levi's wife, an owl shifter who had nearly lost her life to Samir last winter.

"She's fine," Levi said. He shut the car door and

spun in a circle, looking around. Across from my building's parking lot is a road, then the hardware store, a church up the little hill a ways and its parking lot, a park beyond the church, and then a bunch of houses. At noon in the middle of the week, it was quiet, with only a couple cars parked in front of Kim's Hardware.

Levi shook his head as though having a conversation with himself. He still had grease smears on his coveralls and forearms, looking like he'd driven over here after crawling out from under a leaky engine. I didn't see any blood, at least.

"Levi?" I said when he still didn't speak. "You are freaking us out a little."

"Sorry," he said. He came over and waved us toward the table. "I think I fucked up," he added.

Chinese food forgotten, Alek and I sat down across from Levi. I pressed my thigh into Alek's, wanting the reminder that I had a big bad tiger here in case anything was going wrong all over again. My fingers itched to touch my talisman and see if the gem was still in place, but I resisted. It was there, I'd already checked a couple million times just over the course of the morning.

"I was working on, well, it doesn't matter," Levi said. He folded his calloused hands on the table and looked between us with dark, unhappy eyes. "Two guys pulled up in an SUV. I thought they might want help, but soon as I got out there, I smelled they were shifters." He paused and looked around again, as if satisfying himself that we were alone.

We were. It was quiet. No SUVs in sight, if that's what he was worried about.

"So?" I said. "There are a lot of shifters in this town."

"Couple of wolves," Levi said. "Not familiar with them, but that's what I figured, right? I figure they are here because of Freyda being the Alpha and all. Lots of wolves come through, pay respects, talk about whatever wolves talk about."

"None of this explains fuck up," Alek said, raising his eyebrows at Levi.

"They asked about you," Levi said. He tugged on one of the thick plugs in his ear. "I'm not explaining well, sorry. I can't shake the bad feeling I got after I thought about things but maybe I'm crazy."

"You could have called. I do have a phone," I said. It was inside on the counter, I realized, as I patted my pocket and found it empty. But I had finally replaced my cell phone with the most shatter-proof, damage-resistant phone and case I could find. I'd had it for seven months without frying it, falling on it, or someone shooting it. A record for me lately.

"Junebug thought I should come explain in person, plus I wanted to make sure you were all right. Just in case."

"So they asked about me?" I said. What would a couple wolf shifters want with me? I mean, ignoring the part where I kind of blew up their council meeting thingy and killed a former Justice who happened to be a wolf. But Freyda, the new Alpha, had forgiven me for all that since I'd saved her and a lot of others in the process.

"No," Levi said. "They asked about Alek. Said they needed the advice of a Justice but wouldn't really say why. I figured it was personal if they needed a Justice and didn't press. They said they'd heard one was in town."

"They ask for me by name?" Alek said.

"No." Levi shook his head. "I explained that we had a former Justice, but he wasn't doing work for the Council anymore. They said that was okay, they just needed advice. They were really pleasant, which thinking about it rubbed me weird. If they really need a Justice enough to seek one out, why be so calm? No offense, Alek, but I've never heard of anyone seeking a Justice who wasn't utterly desperate or plain suicidal."

"No offense taken," Alek said, inclining his head. His silky white blond hair waved around his face as he stared past Levi into some middle distance. "Death often follows us."

"So you told them where Alek is?" I guessed. I could see why Levi was second-guessing himself. He'd given the wolf shifters a lot of information they might not have had, and if they had violent intentions, that wasn't a good thing. But in Levi's defense, my brain argued, he couldn't know what their intentions were. Maybe they really did need help, and if that was so, Levi had done the right thing.

"Yeah," Levi said. He splayed his hands on the table. "I told them his name and that they could find him at the game shop most likely around noon. I even thought about calling over instead, but it was hot, I had work waiting, and I just didn't think it through. Then as I went back to work, I kept thinking how weird things had felt, running back over their manners and words. I talked to Junebug about it and came here."

"Well, at the risk of inviting trouble, it's all quiet here." I looked around and shrugged. The table was sideways to the lot specifically so nobody had to sit with their back to a parking lot. We all had a decent view of the surroundings to confirm my obvious statement.

"Describe the men?" Alek said.

"Mind if we eat?" I cut in, thinking about my lo mein getting cold. Harper might love cold noodles, but she and I had to agree to disagree on that.

"No, go ahead," Levi said to me as I started unpacking the two Styrofoam lunch boxes. He looked back at Alek and continued, "They were white men, but tanned from being outdoors a lot. Not tall, and probably brothers? They had the same cleft in their chins, I remember noticing that. Nothing too distinct, sorry. Light brown hair, brown eyes I think. Dressed in jeans, both of them. Boots looked well worn, I remember that too. They looked like working men, that's why I figured at first they were guys whose car was having trouble. Nothing threatening about them and no weapons I could see."

"Why did they come to you, did they say?" I asked after I swallowed a lukewarm bit of noodle and cabbage.

"Nope. I didn't ask. Like I said, I wasn't really thinking. Things have been so normal lately, I forgot to think about trouble." Levi sighed.

"There might not be trouble," Alek said. His brow was furrowed, belying his words. "Did they wear rings?" he asked.

I put down my chopsticks and looked at him, worried now more than I'd been before. From his slightly concerned expression, the description of the men had rung a bell in Alek's mind. Slightly concerned on Alek was a panic face on someone else. I felt my own panic face creeping up.

"No," Levi said after he closed his eyes and thought about it for a minute. "No jewelry at all. I think that would have stood out, since they looked like a couple construction workers. I suppose they could have had a necklace hidden under their shirts since they were collared button-downs, but definitely no rings or earrings or anything."

I felt Alek relax as much as saw it in his smoothing brow and I told my adrenaline system to stand down.

"I do not think I know them, then."

"They sounded like people you knew?" I asked.

Alek raised a shoulder in a half shrug and opened his lunch container. "A little, but that was years ago, and they would have rings. It is good these are not those wolves." He smiled, but it wasn't one of his nice smiles. It was more a baring of the teeth that made me really glad he was on my side.

"What did you do to those wolves?" Levi said, unconsciously leaning back from Alek. I didn't blame him.

"I threw their brother off a building," Alek said. "Also, I cut head off their Alpha." He picked up a chicken leg and ripped the meat off the bone with his even, white teeth.

Levi looked from Alek to me. "Is he quoting a Die Hard movie?"

"What is this movie?" Alek looked at me.

"I haven't shown those to him yet," I said. "Bruce Willis," I told Alek. "We can't watch them until Christmas though, cause they are holiday movies."

Levi snorted as Alek shrugged and tore more chicken off his drumstick.

"It's hard to tell when you are joking, Alek," Levi said.

"I do not joke," Alek said. "There was a case years ago, I worked it with another Justice. Little girls going missing, then found half-eaten. The humans were very upset, starting to ask many questions the Council does not want humans asking. We tracked down a pack of wolves, found they were hiding that their Alpha had gone insane. He'd killed some of the pack already for arguing. In fight with Alpha, one of the brothers came and tried to defend. I killed him. He had two other brothers in pack, but they were not present for much of this, so they were allowed to live."

Shifter justice. It's no cake walk.

I looked around. The sun was still shining. Across the parking lot and street, an old man walked out of the hardware store with a cane in one hand and a roll of electric fencing tucked under his other arm. He put the fencing in his trunk, went around the side, opened the door, got in, and drove away. A swallow swooped and looped overhead.

Normal life out there. Eating noodles and discussing murder in here. Two worlds, side by side. This was my life. I scooped another mouthful of noodles up with my chopsticks.

"Good thing it wasn't them," Levi said after a minute of us chewing.

"Good thing," Alek agreed. The look in his eye said he'd still wasn't totally sure.

"Thank you," I said to Levi. "Call if you see them again? Did you get a plate number?"

"No," Levi said. Then he perked up and smiled. "I have that new camera though, outside the shop. It might have caught their plate from the angle they pulled in at. Might even have their faces. I'll copy the video and get it to you?"

"Bring it to the Sheriff's office," Alek said. "I will be back there by two. Rachel might have ideas. She keeps eye on shifters who come through."

That settled, I offered Levi a soda, but he refused and got up, saying he really should get back to work. On instinct, I got up too and went over and hugged him.

"You didn't fuck up," I said softly to him as his arms came around me in surprise, returning the hug with a quick squeeze. "We can't live in high alert mode. It isn't healthy."

"Thanks, Jade," Levi said, squeezing me again.

"You going to look into this?" I asked Alek as I watched Levi drive away.

Silence greeted me and I turned to look at my mate.

He sat with a chicken leg halfway to his mouth, one eyebrow raised.

"Okay," I said. "Stupid question. Just be careful."

"I am always careful," Alek said, looking wounded.

I went back to enjoy lunch with him, but I couldn't shake the feeling that we were in the calm before the storm now. I regretted that thought as soon as it formed, hearing again the smooth whisper of Samir's voice in my mind telling me it was not the calm, but the eye.

The eye of the storm. Even as the thought clicked into place I shoved it away again. "Shut the fuck up," I told the phantom in my head and then I went to enjoy the hell out of my totally normal lunch in the sunlight.

The gem in my D20 talisman was still there, hard under my thumb. Not that I checked because I was worried at all, nope. It was just habit. Only habit.

Alek told me that night he'd reviewed the tapes with Levi, but they hadn't pulled a full plate and the men hadn't been within camera frame. Levi was going to adjust his camera in case they came back and had been all apologies that the video wasn't good for much. He'd installed it mostly for the insurance benefits and visual deterrence. The kind of trouble we had generally wasn't the type that was caught on camera or that you'd take to the human police if it were, so I didn't blame him.

Technology had a lot to recommend it, but preserving secrecy like shifters and other supernaturals have to do makes tech an enemy as much as a friend sometimes. We tend to stay away from cameras.

I spent some quality time early the next morning playing with the wards on my shop and home, making sure they were stable and would warn me about anything non-human entering the facility. It would be annoying, since half the people who came through my shop on a regular basis weren't human, so I'd get humming warnings a lot inside my brain, but I figured a little vigilance now if some kind of shifter trouble was brewing would be worth the headache. Alek and I ate lunch inside two days in a row, despite the beautiful weather.

The second night, trouble arrived, but it wasn't in the form of a wolf shifter.

Alek and I were eating a late dinner after I'd locked up the shop when my wards hummed. Alek tipped his head to one side, listening.

"Car," he said. He rose from the table and went to where his gun was hanging by our unused coats near the door.

"Wards pinged," I said, tugging on my magic, just getting it ready. In case. I'd been tense enough the last couple days that I kind of wanted a fight. Or at least an enemy, if there was one out there, that I could see face to face. I didn't like being worried about a phantom threat.

Footsteps on the stairs. I'd made them nice wrought iron for a reason. Nobody walked up those stairs quietly, not even Alek. We'd tested.

My doorbell rang, the chimes playing the Song of Storms run from *Zelda: Ocarina of Time*. Would evil ring the doorbell? Maybe.

Alek stepped to the side where he would have a clear shot when I opened the door. Which I did, slowly, with my other hand glowing with a readied spell that would slam whatever or whomever was on the landing off it if they were a threat.

A tall white man in a suit stood on the landing. He looked vaguely familiar but I couldn't place where I'd seen him.

"Miss Crow," he said in a polite, even tone, as though I wasn't standing there with a glowing hand and a huge Viking behind me holding a gun. "The Archivist would like to talk to you."

So, not exactly an enemy. Noah Grey, the Archivist, was a vampire, and had been key, if I was being honest, in defeating Samir. He'd helped my find my father, who had helped me get my magic back and shown me who I really was.

But the Archivist was a vampire and well known for selling information to whomever might bid highly enough for it. No matter how he'd helped me, there had always been that nagging feeling inside my gut warning me it wasn't for my sake, but in his own interests. If someday our interests no longer aligned, I wasn't sure what would happen.

Hopefully today wasn't that day.

"I'm not going to Seattle tonight," I said, looking past the suit to where a dark car was parked below.

"He is here," the suit said, "in the car."

I looked back at Alek. My mate had lowered his gun, his finger alongside the trigger. Ready, but not expecting immediate threat. Question was, did I invite the vampire inside my home? Or did I go down and climb into a car with him?

"I'll come down," I said, letting my spell fade as I closed my fist on the magic. "Let me put on shoes."

I closed the door before the suit could answer and went to grab my All-Stars from the shoe bench.

"Watch from the porch?" I asked Alek.

Alek stood there with his gun, looking unhappy. "You are in danger? I thought this vampire helped us?"

"No," I said. "Probably no danger. I just don't

know. I can't read him at all. Besides, why would he show up now if it weren't some kind of trouble?" The only times I'd met Noah were when things were going really poorly in the fight against Samir. Once to get a book from him, once when he rescued me from Boise and helped me find a lot of answers.

I knew the other reason I was nervous. "I owe him a favor," I told Alek. "I think he might have come to collect."

"He will not want something small," Alek agreed with a head shake. He didn't seem surprised by this news. I'd told Alek most of what had happened after I'd turned back time and everyone got split up, including the part where his sister had been hired by the vampire to help me break my biological dad out of jail. I'd sort of glossed over the favor thing, but knowing Alek, he'd put it together anyway.

"Probably not." I stopped the middle of tying my shoe and looked at Alek. "Should I make him get out so I know it's really him? We just have suit guy's word on this." I needed to start thinking like a paranoid survivor again, but it sure sucked.

"Man on porch is human," Alek said. "He was not lying, is easy to read. I would have said something, Jade."

"Thanks," I said, finishing tying my shoe. I stood up and blew Alek a kiss. "Time to go find out what he wants, I guess."

"How will I know if you need me to come break things?" Alek asked as I opened the door.

The suit guy was still standing there, looking slightly annoyed but hiding it behind a façade of professionalism. He was good but that fit. Noah wouldn't hire anyone but the best, I imagined.

I grinned up at the suit guy. "I'll set the car on fire," I said.

Suit guy leaned away from me, his face going even paler. "This way, Miss Crow" he said in a voice slightly higher pitched from how he'd sounded before.

I looked up at Alek as I reached the car. He stood on the small porch, gun in hand but deceptively relaxed. Waiting with the patience of an apex predator. His eyes glinted in the porch light and his hair haloed around his head and shoulders in the evening breeze. It felt good to have back-up. I have him a thumbs-up as suit guy opened the door.

The interior of the car was lit by a dome light only. It was one of those cars modified to have two bench seats facing each other, like you see in mobster movies.

Noah Grey sat on the side facing forward, so I climbed in and took the bench across from him.

"Jade," Noah said. He was the same unnervingly still nondescript man he'd always been.

The suit closed the door behind me. There was some kind of covering on the windows that made the interior dark as a crypt. The car had its air conditioning running, which made it feel even more like slipping into a tomb, or at least that's what my over-imaginative brain was telling me. My skin broke out in goosebumps.

"Archivist," I said, figuring being moderately polite wouldn't hurt me. "Long drive from Seattle. What do you want?" There was polite, and then there was engaging in small talk with a vampire. I drew the line somewhere, plus I'm terrible at small talk with anyone.

"I would like to call in my favor," Noah said. A smile moved his lips into a slight curve but it didn't touch his eyes.

"Okay?" My stomach twisted into a rope even as my heart played a little excited tap dance beat.

"I inherited a house," he continued. "It used to belong to a magic user. No," he added, seeing the look on my face, "not Samir's place. Nobody has found his home that I've heard about." He said it in a way that made it clear he expected he would. Being the Archivist, a gatherer of knowledge and magical items from all over the planet, I figured he was right.

That he was looking was news to me, but I'd wondered about what had happened to Samir's cache of magic books, journals, and other things he'd gathered over his lifetime. It was all out there somewhere, a dangerous treasure trove waiting for someone to unlock it. I hoped it was hidden very, very well.

"Waiting to hear how it involves me, then," I said, rubbing my palms on the bench. The seats were some kind of buttery soft leather. They hadn't had anything this nice in the surplus office supply depot I used to refurbish my store.

"There might be magical items in there that are dangerous or just unknown. Books, weapons, and so on. I know you have done this kind of work for Ciaran. It should be simple, but of course, I cannot promise it will be completely safe. There is likely magic involved, after all." Noah stared evenly at me.

The job sounded simple enough. Go to some house, figure out what was and wasn't magical. Try to neutralize anything dangerous or unknown. I'd done similar, as he'd said. Should be easy enough. Seemed almost too simple to waste a carte blanche kind of favor from a half-dragon sorceress on. Which was the problem I was having.

"So you drove all the way from Seattle to meet me instead of picking up a phone. To ask me to go to a house and do a little magic sniffing around the stuff inside? And after I do that, we're even?" I folded my arms, giving him my best skeptical look.

"You can hang up a phone," Noah said. "Or ignore a call. Yes, when you have done this task to my satisfaction, we are even, as you say."

The thing about dealing with supernatural entities is you have to really listen to the details, and to what they don't say. Done this task to his satisfaction? That was some crazy politician-level doublespeak if I'd ever heard it. Talk about leaving the door wide open for further demands.

If he was going to show up and give me a quest, couldn't it at least have been something straightforward. Clean out a warren of demonic something-or-others. Torch the lair of an enemy vampire. Save Timmy from the well. Instead I got the "go to this house, look at antiques" quest with a huge open question at the end of "what if I find something really bad?"

"What if I find something really dangerous?" I asked. I wasn't sure how I felt about handing something over to Noah, where it might be resold to the highest bidder or used against me someday.

"I understand that concern," Noah said. He inclined his head, the gesture slow and deliberate. He'd been practicing his humanity in front of a mirror for a lot of decades, I guessed. "If that happens, we can discuss how to dispose of said item. I am not allergic to compromise, if you will remember."

"Am I supposed to look for something in particular?" I asked.

"There might be some anatomy jars with things the public should not have." Noah lifted his shoulders in what would have been a casual shrug if it didn't look like he was thinking "flex shoulders now" while doing it.

"Anatomy jars? What kind of magic user lived there?" This was sounding more sketchy by the minute.

"Minor warlock," he said. "He collected many things, I am told. But he will not trouble you." His eyes bored into me, as though daring me to ask more.

A warlock. I'd dealt with one of those before. They were basically like male witches. Not born with magic like a sorcerer but just a human who had acquired it through spell book rituals or a powerful item or the like.

"So we'll do this together?" I said. I wasn't sure I wanted him along, depending on what I found, but it was his house. Probably.

"No," Noah answered with a slight shake of his head. "I think it best if you go in and make sure it is safe before I or my people tread there."

I sighed. I did have to remember that he'd helped me stop Samir from turning into a god. I knew my suspicions were a little unfair. It was hard to trust even now, with my greatest enemy defeated. I wanted to ask more questions, to shake his solemn ass until he told me whatever he wasn't telling me, but I had a feeling it wouldn't do any good. Facts were that I owed him and this was how he wanted to be repaid. Maybe I shouldn't look the gift-horse in the mouth.

"Where's the house?" I asked.

"About three hours drive from here. It should not take you more than a day to inventory. Damien will give you all the information. I would prefer this done as soon as possible since I would like to sell the house once I know it is safe to do so."

That explanation made sense, though I wondered how and why he'd gotten it in the first place if he just wanted to sell it off again. Maybe someone lost a bet. Or maybe that warlock had owed him a favor and not paid up.

With that sobering thought, I mentally reviewed my schedule. "I have to figure out coverage for the store," I said, which mostly meant calling Lara and begging her to work a longer day either Sat or Sun. "So this weekend is the soonest I can do it."

I was also thinking about how to keep this from my friends. I'd have to tell Alek, and he'd probably come along, but if there were magic devices in this place, having a full crew with me might be more trouble than help. On the other hand, I could see an adventure away from Wylde being good for us.

It was a pretty simple task, after all. I shoved away the nagging feelings of doubt again.

Noah was very quiet for a moment and I wished I could read his expression, but trying to glean something from his face was like looking at a plaster bust of a Roman emperor and asking it for the time.

"That will do," he said in a resigned tone, as though waiting two days would be a chore. "No later than that."

I saw no signal, but suit guy opened the door at that point. I took the hint that the discussion was over. Suit guy had a folder in his hand, so I guessed he was the Damien that Noah had referred to.

"Thanks, Damien," I said, flashing him a toothy smile as I took the folder. "I'll be in touch," I called back into the car at Noah. He made no reply.

I clanged up the iron steps to where Alek waited. Noah's car drove away beneath us as we watched. When I couldn't see headlights anymore, we went inside.

"What does he want?" Alek asked as I put the folder on the table among our half-eaten steaks and twice-baked potatoes.

"I can't be sure," I said. Then I added a thought, voicing the only idea that made any sense given that weird conversation just now, "but I think the Archivist wants me to rob a house."

Alek wasn't happy with my plan for us to drive out and take care of this quietly, but he understood that I didn't want my friends involved in what might be not only dangerous, but illegal. If the human cops showed up, it'd be a lot easier to pull some invisibility magic or something to cover two people rather than five. I figured Harper, Levi, and Ezee would forgive me later, though I knew I'd get a lecture from them about being over-protective and not accepting help. I was supposed to have turned over a new leaf and all that when it came to being up front about things with them.

New leaves are great and all, but this was either going to be a far more dangerous mission than it appeared or it was going to be a super boring romp through what appeared to be, from the single picture in the file, a two story Elizabethan-style home plunked down in the literal middle of nowhere. What I knew about the area, which wasn't much since it was definitely in the "drive through quickly" category, was it was rocky, empty, and brown most of the year. For all I knew, this would be the most boring weekend day trip anyone has taken.

I wouldn't have even taken Alek with me, but I kind of wanted someone to drive and I didn't think I could talk him out of it anyway. After crashing my car into a moose earlier this year, I was still kind of leery of being behind the wheel, though I was overcoming it in small bursts of courage. I know, I know. Phenomenal cosmic powers, scared of getting behind a wheel after a single car wreck. To be fair, I thought I'd killed Alek in that wreck, so I felt like my fears were a little justified. I'd seen him covered in blood and presumed dead way too many times since we'd met. Never again wouldn't be far enough away for my comfort.

We'd decided on Saturday, since that was the best day for Lara to cover. I hated lying to my friends, but fortunately none of them asked on Thursday night at game what the plans were for the weekend. I think they just assumed they were the same as ever, and I figured I'd rather ask forgiveness than permission so I let them assume we'd be doing Diablo after hours on Saturday. With any luck, Alek and I could be back by late evening. It seemed obvious from my conversation with the Archivist that what he really wanted was whatever was in those anatomy jars I might or might not find. I had to admit I was dying of curiosity about what a vampire would want with a fermented pig fetus or whatever it would be.

"Maybe it's an alien," I speculated as Alek and I went outside to eat lunch on Friday afternoon.

He'd come a little later than usual, having been delayed by a prank call at one of the hotels that he'd gone to check out with Sheriff Lee. We'd decided to eat outside after the total lack of anything happening by whoever those two wolves were. They hadn't contacted the shop or approached Alek. Their SUV, which the partial plate hadn't been able to identify, hadn't been reported by anyone and I'd kept an eye out for it and seen nothing either. My wards were now extended to include the parking lot, as annoying as that was when half the shifters in town parked back there at various times to go into Brie's bakery. My wards had been lightly buzzing all morning. The lunch rush was over and the afternoon coffee rush wouldn't start for a while, so only my car, Brie's bakery van, and a couple local cars I couldn't name the owners of but who I'd recognize on sight as being local were the only ones back there. Tourists and visitors always parked in front since the way around to the back lot wasn't obvious if you didn't know the town well.

I wished there was a way to hone my wards to only identify people who were threats, but I had no idea how to even begin doing something that complex. If I got it wrong, it might backfire horribly. I wasn't a ward specialist. More of a fireball and ask questions later kind of sorceress. We all have our strengths, I guess.

"Maybe it is trap," Alek said, raining on my speculation parade. He was still unhappy about doing this at all with so little information.

"Noah helped me," I pointed out. "Why do that?"

"For that," he said, motioning at my D20 with his ham sandwich. A piece of lettuce slipped out and splorked onto the table with a wet, mustardy slap.

"What good would it do him?" I said, rubbing the gem in the 1 spot on the polyhedral die. "He can't eat it and gain Samir's power."

"Are you the last sorcerer?" Alek asked.

I saw his point, but I stubbornly refused to make it for him. "If a sorcerer eats this we get boom! Magic apocalypse. Noah doesn't want that. Humans might think vampires are sexy now, but if they learned all that shit was real? Fuck knows what they'd do, and there are a lot of them. They breed faster than we do and have nukes, remember? I trust his sense of self-preservation if nothing else."

I didn't admit to him that there were nights when I awoke from my nightmares and wondered if it would be so awful. If ripping open the seals and letting all the weird shit in the world come to light, letting gods back in to deal with this messy planet wouldn't be worth getting a little sleep at night knowing that Samir was gone forever. As long as I held him here in limbo, there was always the chance he'd pull a Darth Vader on me.

Fortunately caffeine and sanity always stopped me from doing something that reckless. For now.

"Perhaps. I still do not like this." Alek shook his head and went back to his sandwich.

There was no good response since we were going anyway. I didn't favor being on the Archivists shit list. I picked at my chips and looked around the neighborhood. A few fluffy white clouds marred the impossibly blue skies but the sun was out, the air was cooler than the last few days but still pleasant teeshirt weather. The hardware store looked deserted, but someone was parked up at the church.

I dropped my chip and stood up, raising my arm to block the glare of the sun.

"That look like a black SUV to you?" I asked Alek. I started to move to the left as I realized I'd blocked his view by standing where I was.

Hot pain punched into my gut and folded me over even as it shoved me backward and down. *Not again*, I thought. I knew what this was. Bullet. I fucking hate getting shot.

I reached for my magic through the white hot agony burning its way into me and started to get a shield up. "Alek," I yelled in warning. He was quick, he'd get down behind me. I hoped he had his gun on him. I couldn't remember if he'd left it inside.

Somewhere in the back of my mind I registered the sound of the second shot but my shield came up and I didn't feel a second bullet. I turned and started trying to crawl back toward where Alek had flattened himself onto the ground by the table. Blood squelched and spurted between my fingers as I clutched at the wound. The shooter wasn't fucking around. This was a serious caliber. I'd gotten lucky they'd hit through the very side of my abdomen and missed my spine.

"Alek," I said as I crawled toward him. "Alek, they are behind us." My vision was dimmed by the pain and the strain of keeping the magic going in its bubble around us. He'd dropped down onto his side, facing away from me. Away from the threat. Had he not seen where the bullet had come from? Did he see something else the other direction?

Blood, dark red and flowing like water toward a storm drain. It was everywhere around him, under him.

I shoved myself over the patio through the hot, slippery mess and reached Alek's side. He had his hands over his throat, blood gushing between his clutching fingers. His ice-blue eyes were white and wide with panic and pain.

Somewhere in my head I knew I was screaming. The sound was far away, like it was coming from another throat. I heard the squeal of tires behind me in the distance and twisted in time to see the SUV drive past. Something hit my shield like a freight train but my magic, running on instinct born of training, held it off. Then the SUV was gone before my brain could turn the magic on the attack, and I was alone with all the blood.

I knew my wound wasn't fatal no matter how much pain I was in. My hands found Alek's and I pressed them around his, trying to staunch the blood flow. His eyes were still wide open, unblinking, but his heart was still beating, pumping all that blood right out onto the cement. His hands moved, falling away as his eyes started to flutter closed. Beneath my fingers I saw gaping flesh, like a horror movie nightmare come to life.

"Shift," I told him. "Shift." It was his only chance. I didn't know how to heal with my magic. This was way out of my skillset.

Alek's eyes closed. The gush of blood beneath my hands started to slow as his heart quit on him.

Reaching for my magic, I took the only shot I could to try to save him.

I used Tess's magic and knowledge to slow time. I couldn't risk trying to turn it backward again and I didn't have the power of ley lines to help me do that even if I wanted to, which I admit I desperately did. I'd sworn off time magic completely after that incident, but this was the very definition of extenuating circumstances.

I felt the air around me still. All noise ceased. Alek's hideous gurgling breaths had already slowed to nothing. I tried to remember how I'd reached him before, when he was poisoned. I pushed magic at his heart in a desperate bid to make it beat just a little longer.

"Shift," I told him. "Shift."

His eyes fluttered and his lips folded back from his bloody teeth in a snarl. Then there was tiger beneath my hands, fur instead of flesh. His chest heaved and fell, heaved and fell. His eyes were closed again and though I tried, I could get no response.

But he breathed. I leaned in against him and listened for his heart. Faint but there, deep within his huge chest. Tiger-Alek had no wound in his neck, but I had no idea how long it would take him to heal. If he healed. I pushed that thought away. At least he wasn't bleeding out here in the mortal world anymore. I'd take whatever small victories I could.

Movement beyond the shimmering bubble of slowed time around us caught my eye. Lara's form hovered there. She was smart enough not to walk into the spell.

I didn't want to let go of the magic. If time sped up, would Alek hang on? I couldn't keep us there forever. Doing this much on top of the shield and being injured myself was already draining the snot out of me. The bile? I felt the blood loss taking its toll on my mental focus.

With a promise to the Universe that I'd be the best

person possible going forward if they'd just save Alek, I dropped the time spell. Wind and noise rushed in on me as the breath I hadn't realized I'd been holding gasped out. Pain radiated from my side, punching me anew with every beat of my own heart, even though a quick glance showed the bleeding was already slowing.

"Holy mother of god, Jade. Jade. Do I call Nine-one-one?" Lara's voice was loud in my ears and I winced.

"No," I managed to gasp out. "Vivian. Sheriff Lee, too," I added, thinking quickly.

"I'll close the store. Nobody is inside." Lara turned and ran back in.

Brie, her red curls fighting free of her bun, ran out the back of her bakery next door, took one look at me kneeling beside Alek, and made a motion with her hand I couldn't parse, and ran back inside. I was lucky none of her regulars had come out to see what the screaming was about. If anyone came to investigate the sound of gunshots or a woman yelling bloody murder, we were in trouble.

I had a hole in my side that wasn't bleeding anymore but was still an open wound, or so the quick glance that turned my stomach told me. I was kneeling next to a twelve-foot long white tiger, both of us in a giant pool of blood that was already turning black at the edges in the sunshine. The human citizens of Wylde are remarkably good at turning a blind eye to weird shit, but the scene there might have been asking too much. I didn't want to move, afraid if I took my hands off Alek's body he would quit breathing while I wasn't looking.

Ciaran, my leprechaun neighbor, and Brie, came to my rescue. Brie had gone around the front of our block to Ciaran and they came out the back carrying a huge Shoji screen. It was big enough to mostly block the direct view of Alek from the road.

"What happened?" Ciaran asked as they got it up.

"Someone shot us," I said. Those shifters that Levi had talked to, but I didn't say that. We'd hash out who and how to hunt them down and make them wish they'd never been born later. "Alek was hit in the throat. Lara's calling Vivian." I didn't know what the town vet could do, but she'd at least come here and maybe say reassuring things. She knew more about what a shifter could heal than any of us.

"What about you?" Brie said, crouching beside me, not seeming to care that her bright blue tennis shoes were now standing in a pool of blood.

"Hit me in the side, I'll live." I wished they'd shot me in the throat and Alek in the side. We'd stand a better chance that way.

Now that the adrenaline was fading and I could replay the event in my head, things weren't adding up. They'd shot me low and to the side. I could almost believe they'd aimed center mass and had shitty aim, but their hit on Alek was a smaller target than his chest, and direct.

Keeping my hands on Alek's side, I turned and looked toward the church. It was up a hill, giving the shooter a higher vantage, but hundreds of yards away. Not an easy shot, but it gave them a straight line down to where we ate lunch. The awning was high enough that it wouldn't interfere.

I'd been in the way, I realized. That was why they'd shot me first. A shot aimed to cripple and drop me. Alek had been moving, reacting more quickly than they expected. That's why the shot hit his throat and a little to the side, the only thing that saved his life. It should have hit him in the head. Might have, if he'd been just a fraction slower to react to the first and already on alert due to me moving to see the SUV more

ANNIE BELLET

clearly. But why not shoot us earlier? Maybe the SUV arriving was what had caught my eye. I knew some questions might never have answers.

Once I got my hands on them, I was going to be asking different questions. If I bothered asking anything at all before turning them into wolf bbq.

Brie gently pulled away the teeshirt from my wound and I hissed.

"It's closing," she said. "Bullet went through."

"Told you, I'll heal." I tried to shrug her off but that sent a new spike of pain through me. I hate getting shot. Bullet wounds are literally the worst. The worst.

Lara saved me from more prodding by coming back outside. She nodded cautiously to Brie and Ciaran. She didn't know them as anything other than the people who owned shops to either side of mine.

"They're cool," I told her, meaning they weren't going to freak about supernatural stuff. I made a mental note to have the "Brie is a goddess and Ciaran is a leprechaun" talk with her later.

"Vivian is on her way. Couldn't get to the Sheriff, they wouldn't put me through. I left a message that Alek needs her at the place he has lunch as soon as possible. I hope that was vague enough but still gets her attention?" Her eyes kept darting between me and Alek's body. She kept back, right at the doorway.

"He's breathing," I told her. I felt him doing it, slow, almost barely there breaths, under my fingers.

"I can hear it," she said. "What happened?"

"Shot in the throat, I'll explain when Vivian gets here."

"Throat?" Lara said. Her brow furrowed. "That's, uh. I'll go make sure they come around back. I told them to."

"Them?" Brie said as she straightened up.

"Harper was who I got through to at the vet's office, so…" Lara trailed off, looking at me again.

If Harper was coming, she'd be on the phone to Levi and Ezee on the way. If there was trouble, my gang would be in the thick of it before I could say anything. I held back a sigh because doing so would likely hurt too much. There was no keeping them away from this.

If Alek lived, I didn't care. I'd let them all take vengeance alongside me. I knew how shifter justice worked and I was ready to throw in.

"Thanks, Lara," I said. She seemed very calm. Tense, but not freaking out. I appreciated that. I decided she needed a raise. Of course, that depended on if she even wanted to work here after today. If she didn't, I wouldn't blame her.

I heard a car coming and stood up, peering around the screen. The Sheriff's brown SUV came down the street behind my shop at a quick but not alarming pace, her lights off. Rachel Lee pulled in and jumped out almost as soon as she cut the engine, her nostrils flaring as she caught the smell of blood. Rachel was a stocky wolf shifter and had been our sheriff for longer than I'd been in Wylde.

She came around the wooden screen and saw Alek, then looked at me as I crouched back down beside him. Her eyes widened a smidge but that was her only reaction.

"What happened?" she asked.

"I think those two wolves that talked to Levi shot us," I said. The pain my side was fading out to almost manageable levels now and I could breathe without feeling like I was getting stabbed over and over. "Alek took one in the throat."

"Let me move my vehicle to block more of this from the road," Rachel said. She turned and went to do that, coming back quickly after she'd maneuvered her vehicle around to cover the side where the table was and the screen didn't quite reach.

I knelt and kept my hands on Alek's side, wondering what was taking Vivian so damn long.

"We've been getting prank calls about gunfire for two days now, all over the county," Rachel said as she came back over. "When this one came in, I figured it was near your shop and I was going to come get Alek anyway, so I came."

"Lucky," I muttered. Those calls couldn't be coincidence and from Rachel's face, she was thinking what I was thinking. Someone had set it up, probably the people who shot us, so that when gunfire right in the middle of town was reported, nobody would take it that seriously given all the false reports.

Wolves crying wolf. It would have almost been funny, if I hadn't been kneeling in a pool of blood wondering if the love of my life was going to stop breathing any second.

"What happened?" Harper slammed out the back door of my shop and stopped, staring with open mouth. Her lips went back in a snarl as she looked around for a threat after taking in the scene.

Vivian ducked out around her and walked right

through the blood with hesitation.

"You okay?" she said to me.

"Shot in my lower side, but it's healing," I said. "Alek was hit in the throat. He shifted but he's barely breathing."

"Shot? Who shot you?" Harper said, her voice now almost a growl.

"Azalea, come stand over here with us," Ciaran said, using Harper's proper name to get her attention. "Let the doc do her work."

"I'm okay," I repeated to her as she edged by Alek's body.

Vivian pulled out a stethoscope and started listening to Alek's heart. More tires on roadway noise. I couldn't see around the screen to know who it was, but Levi's voice told me a second later. Both him and Junebug, his wife, appeared around the side of the screen and froze, looking at us all.

This was getting to be too many people. I couldn't handle it all, them staring and asking questions. I felt like a goldfish or a zoo exhibit.

"Too many people," I said aloud. "Please." I was trying to hold it all together, watching Vivian's face for any sign of news before she spoke, but she just kept listening, a tight frown on her lips. Beneath my hands, Alek still breathed, the breaths so subtle that without my fingers buried in his fur, I might have missed the rise and fall of his huge chest.

"Come on," Brie said. "All of you besides the Sheriff and the doctor. Let's go into my shop before we drawn a human crowd, eh?"

Nobody wanted to go, Levi strenuously insisting it was his fault and he should stay in case there was more trouble.

"Go," I yelled at them, regretting it as soon as I did because it caused my side and gut to seize with pain as I pushed air out of my diaphragm too quickly.

They went. Rachel stood guard at the edge of the screen, her hand casually on her gun butt, eyes scanning the street. Vivian sat back on her heels and looked at me across Alek's body.

"He's alive," she said. "All this blood." She shook her head. "Shifting probably saved him."

"Probably?" I said, not liking the sound of that. Admittedly, I wouldn't like the sound of anything short of "it's a miracle he's fine and should wake up any second to tell you so himself."

"He's not dead yet. That's a good sign. His heartbeat

is very slow and his breathing is not consistent. I can't promise he'll live, Jade. But I can guess that he will. Alek is the strongest shifter I've ever known. That poison should have killed him last year. If he could pull through that, he can pull through this." Vivian's expression was hopeful, her gaze steady as she met my eyes.

"Can we move him?" I asked, looking away from her and around the lot. "They might come back if they think the job isn't done. Plus it's Friday and that's a busy evening. He's too exposed out here."

"Moving him won't hurt him further. It's a question now of if he can heal his body in the other world." She waved her hand in a vague gesture meant to denote the place that shifters stored their animal or human forms, whichever they weren't using. Some of them called it the "Between" and some called it the "Veil" and some just the "other world" or "other place."

"Can we move him?" Sheriff Lee asked. "I don't think he'll fit through your back door here and your apartment is two flights up."

I had an elevator, well, a lift really, installed inside, but it only went from ground floor to the gaming rooms, not to my apartment. I'd done it so people with mobility issues could still access the gaming rooms. I hadn't thought through access to the top floor, evidently. Something I'd have to fix.

"He'll fit through that door," I said, pointing upward, though the awning hid where I was pointing. The stairs were to the right of me. Maybe if enough of us lifted at the same time we could do it? Shifters were very strong and I had a small force of them inside Brie's now.

The mental image of us trying to push Alek's giant tiger body up my stairs like people moving an unwieldly piece of furniture nixed that idea quickly. I reluctantly took my hands off his fur and stood up, wincing. A glance downward told me the bullet wound was almost closed. I wished I could impart some of my near-immortality into Alek. If wishes were horses we'd all win the Kentucky Derby.

The afternoon quiet held. No cars. Nobody at the church or hardware store. I had an idea that was probably crazy, but as long as no normals saw me, we'd be just fine.

"Get my keys," I told Rachel. "Inside the shop, next to the register."

She went and got them and then unlocked the

apartment door as I instructed and waited patiently, holding it open.

"What are you going to do?" Vivian asked me.

"Fly," I said. "Quiet, I need to concentrate."

I closed my eyes and visualized exactly what I wanted to do. I'd never really done this before, but I'd used similar techniques in DnD games, so how tough could it be? I pushed down the rising fear that I'd fuck this up and drop my lover to his death two stories below.

What I needed was a mix of a fly spell with Levitation, and a bit of Tenser's Floating Disk. I visualized my magic like giant, stiff cargo netting wrapping around Alek's body, letting the magic slide in a controlled fashion from my outstretched hands and wrap gently around him. Gentle magic isn't my strong suit, but damned if I wasn't going to learn a new trick today if I had to. I heard Vivian gasp and figured it must be working since I didn't smell burning fur.

With another deep breath that send a stabbing reminder through my side, I opened my eyes. Pale purple lines of power flowed from my hands like giant cables and wove around tiger-Alek, turning his white fur to violet in their magic light. Using myself as the anchor point, I gave my magic net a shove upward. Alek lifted about two feet off the ground, the lines holding him mostly rigid and stable. Carefully I walked backward. Vivian scrambled to move the Shoji screen out of our way as I floated Alek out from under the awning.

I'd installed an extra wide front door at the top of the landing so that Alek could get in and out if he needed to in tiger form, since with our lives we never knew what would happen. I was pretty sure he would fit even laying down with his legs out, but if he didn't, I had built the netting around him in a way that I was fairly sure I could rotate him if needed.

Once out from under the awning, I pushed us both into the air. I prayed our luck would hold because right now there was a floating, glowing twelve-foot long tiger and a woman with giant purple cables around her body and in her hands driving him before her like a chariot. The YouTube video would have been crazy. I shoved aside my scattered thoughts and worries, keeping tight hold of my magic as I guided Alek slowly toward the door once I had us level with the top deck. I'd left off railings despite recommended building codes for reasons not exactly identical to this, but with a quick escape of a large tiger in mind if it had to happen. A lifetime of running from Samir had trained me to always build with easy escape routes in mind.

Rachel flattened herself against the inside wall to make the opening as big as possible as I carefully guided Alek through. I let my feet come down onto the landing and walked in after him, my eyes fixed on Alek's body. The magic in my hands felt thinner by the moment as fatigue and injury started to catch up to me and the edges of my vision dimmed. I couldn't drop him yet. Not gonna happen. I gritted my teeth and clutched at the purple cords like they were real cables, strengthening them with sheer will.

I heard Vivian coming up the iron steps behind me as I floated Alek into the living room and finally, slowly, lowered him down to the floor. I let go of the magic as he settled and rushed to his side. For a terrible moment I felt no movement, no breath. Then his fur beneath my panicking hands lifted and dropped. Vivian knelt and pressed her face against him, not even bothering with her stethoscope, just using her wolf-shifter hearing.

"Still beating," she said. She made an attempt at a smile. "I'll get an IV into him, get him fluids to help replace the blood. I think he'll make it, Jade. I really do."

I lay down, letting exhaustion, both physical and emotional, take over. Pressing my face into Alek's shoulder, I curled against him. He would live, damn it all, because I couldn't imagine him not living. He would live, and when he woke I was going to go find those two wolves and teach them why the world was terrified of sorcerers. Teach them why nobody messes with my family. Never ever again.

I must have dozed off because I didn't remember everyone arriving in my house. I swallowed the taste of sleep from my mouth as the sound of low voices carried to me. My head was still on Alek's shoulder, though it had slipped down to mostly pillow on his foreleg. I shoved my hands into his fur and felt him breathing. His breathing was steadier. His breaths moved his chest like they should have, I thought, hoping it wasn't just my imagination. I wiggled down and pressed my cheek to his side. His heart was beating strongly enough for me to hear it now. That wasn't my imagination.

"He's doing better," Vivian said.

I sat up and saw her sitting crosslegged on the floor on Alek's other side. She had a couple throw pillows behind her so she could lean on the chair that Harper was perched in.

"How're you?" Harper asked me as I raised my gaze to meet her worried green eyes.

"I don't know," I said. "How long did I sleep?" I turned to look out the window and saw it was dark.

"It's nearly midnight," she said. "We thought you should rest."

"That's a long time," I said, sitting up more. I felt my stomach where the bullet had hit me. There was only a divot on either side now, the flesh there white against my brown skin. The scar would be gone in a day or so, I knew. I took a couple deep breaths and flexed the sad excuse I had for abdominal muscles. No pain.

Junebug came out of my bathroom, wiping her hands on her long, hand-stitched skirt.

"I sent Levi and his brother for snacks," she said, smiling at me. "Not a lot here that's ready-made. Brie and Ciaran said to call if you need them, but they are planning on staying up and keeping an eye out. Lara is sleeping downstairs on one of the game room couches in case she's needed. Sheriff Lee is going to be sending deputies on drive-by all night long and she's looking for that SUV. I think that's all you missed."

My throat got tight and my eyes felt a little watery as I smiled back at her. I had good friends. Then a thought occurred to me, something I'd thought about in passing before I'd crashed.

"Anybody find any of the bullets? I know they are probably pancaked or fragmented." I wasn't sure it would be enough to run a tracking spell, but I was willing to try.

"Lara and Brie hosed down the lot to get rid of the blood. Maybe ask them?" Harper said.

I stroked my hands through Alek's fur and sighed. "Hopefully she'll still want to work here." I reluctantly got to my feet, stretching sore muscles. I looked down at Alek.

"Go shower and change," Vivian said, reading my mind. "He's still alive, Jade, and his vitals are stronger. He's going to make it, I promise."

"I wish he'd wake up," I muttered. I wasn't going to believe he'd be okay until he shifted and told me so himself.

"He needs rest now. It might be another day or more

before he wakes, and longer before he can safely shift." Vivian scritched Alek's ears in a way nobody but me would have dared when he was awake. She was a vet, after all. I imagined she was dealing with him the way she dealt with all her patients. I hoped she was right about his health, but I'd never seen reason to doubt her before. Vivian didn't talk shit or sugarcoat. It wasn't her way.

I showered, pulled on clean clothing, and went to see if my employee was still sane and to let her know she could go and sleep in a real bed if she wanted.

Lara was curled up on one of the couches in the casual gaming room with a sleeping bag under her. It was too warm to really need it. She was awake, or I would have slipped out again, with the light on. She was reading from one of the fantasy novels I kept a small stock of near the counter.

"Hey," she said. "How's Alek?"

"He's doing better. Hasn't woken up yet but Vivian is optimistic."

"Should we start one of those workplace counters? It's been zero days since someone tried to kill you?" She grinned at me, her shoulders tense as she sat up and crossed her legs. Lara was clearly trying to break the ice a little. I appreciated that.

"I had a good streak going," I said in my defense. "Nobody has tried the whole time you worked here or for like months before that."

"I missed all the fun a year ago, but I've heard some stories. Coyotes have good eavesdropping skills." She said coyotes with only two syllables.

"Sorry about today," I said, turning a chair around so I could sit facing her. "I totally understand if you want to find something else."

Lara shrugged. "My mom's an emergency room doctor and my uncle is a professional hunter. I'm not freaked out by blood and stuff, if that's what you mean."

"They coyotes too?"

"Bears. I'm the odd one out. Prof Chapowits says that's usually how it is with coyote shifters. We just manifest our animal half without regard to tradition or bloodline," Lara said, still grinning. Then she sobered a little, her grin dropping to a small smile. "Look, Jade. I am serious. I heard what happened, and the Prof filled in some gaps. Why you had to rebuild the whole block and stuff. I know working here might not be the safest thing, but it's cool. Being a shifter isn't safe either. Nor is being black, when you get down to it. I don't mind risk."

"You can't change who you are," I said. "But this is a risk you could avoid. I didn't think there would be more trouble, but I see now that was probably short-sighted of me. Trouble and I are forever intertwined."

"Or you live in a place with lots of ley lines, a huge number of shifters, and probably things I don't even know about. Would you say Buffy attracted trouble? Or was it just that she lived on a Hellmouth?"

She was using Buffy as an example in a logical argument. I shook my head. I didn't want anyone hurt, but it was hard to keep trying to convince her to go when she clearly belonged. Lara was one of our tribe, as Harper would say.

"I give up," I said. "But seriously, if things get too weird or dangerous, quit any time. I won't blame you."

"Thanks, I'll keep it in mind." Lara dropped her hands onto her crossed ankles. "I'm still working all day, yeah? You gonna do that thing?"

It took me a minute to remember what she was talking about. Noah's house. Shit.

"No," I said, my brain scrambling over how I was going to explain that to the vampire. He'd have to wait. I wasn't leaving Alek to go rob some house. Not until I had taken those would-be killers out of the picture. Which reminded me why I came down here in the first place. "Did you find any bullet fragments or casings or anything when you were cleaning up outside? Do you know if Brie did?"

"We hosed the lot down pretty good," Lara said with a head shake. "Sorry."

"It's okay. It was a long shot anyway," I said. I got to my feet. "You don't have to stay if you want to sleep in a real bed."

"Nah, I'm good," she said. "I'll crash and open the store in the morning unless you tell me otherwise."

"I'll let you know if anything changes," I said. "Thank you."

I went down the back steps and out and around to my place, wondering why I hadn't put a damn door from my place into the store. Separation of work and home life, I supposed.

Ezee and Levi were back, sitting with Harper and Junebug at my dining room table with a pile of snacks in front of them. The only thing open this late in Wylde were bars and our Quickmart. From the fun-size bags of chips, packages of Hostess cake products, and six-pack of ice tea, they'd opted for the latter.

My cell phone sat in front of Ezee. I didn't remember leaving it there.

"You got a call. I figured it was late so maybe it was important. Blocked number," Ezee said. All four of them were looking at me with quizzical faces.

I walked past them and looked at Alek. I'd deal with people answering my phone without permission in a minute. I had no idea who would call anyway.

"He's fine," Vivian said. She had a bag of Fritos in her hands and had moved up to the chair Harper had vacated.

I nodded and went back to the table, pulling out a chair. I grabbed a bag of kettle chips and looked at Ezee. "So?"

"It was the Archivist," he said, that weird tone still in his voice. "He said to wish you and Alek good luck at the house today."

I was sure the expectant silence that followed was the subsonic noise the proverbial cat made as it shot out of the proverbial bag and right into orbit.

"Give me my phone," I said, abandoning the chips even though I was starving. Noah might have called from a blocked number, but I had another number for him. It was worth a try anyway.

"Jade?" Levi said as Ezee slid me the cell.

"I'll explain in a second," I said. I raised my hand

for silence as I found the number in my saved contacts under "Lestat" and hit send.

He picked up on the second ring. "Jade."

"It's off," I said. "Your house is going to have to wait. Someone shot me today and Alek is still hurt." No point wasting time making nice before I broke the news to him, I figured.

There was a long silence that made me wonder if the line had gone dead. Then Noah spoke in a chilled, clipped tone. "It must happen this weekend. There can be no delay."

"It's not going to happen," I said. "Whoever shot us is still out there and until Alek is awake and those bastards are dead, my focus is here, not looking for magical objects in some house."

I saw Harper mouth "looking for magical objects" at Levi with a questioning tilt of her head and Levi giving her the wide-eyed, frowning faced "I dunno" look back. Yep. Cat was firmly traveling beyond orbit and into the Kupier belt any minute now.

"You owe me, Jade Crow," the pissed off vampire on the phone was saying.

"So I'll still owe you. I'm hanging up now," I said. Great. Another enemy.

"Wait," Noah said, a note of panic in his voice that shocked me into putting the phone back to my ear. "Do you know who shot at you?"

"No," I said. "We're looking for them."

"I am good at finding things. At getting information. Give me all the information you have and I will find them for you. If you do the job today, as promised."

"What about if I do it tomorrow?" Sunday would be better, give Alek another day to recover and maybe wake up.

"Today. As promised." Noah's tone was harder than diamonds.

I held the phone away from my face, took a deep breath and exhaled slowly. I looked over at the hulking form of tiger-Alek sleeping. There was what I wanted in life, I was learning, and then there was reality. I wanted to tell the vampire to stick it where the sun don't shine, then pull some crazy awesome magic stuff and find those bastards myself, and end them shifter Justice style, hopefully with my badass, powerful and fully operational shifter Justice mate at my side.

Reality was that we had thin leads, Alek was hurt and down for who knew how long, and I really couldn't afford to make another enemy right now, especially not one as powerful as the Archivist. Reality was also that there was no way I was going to talk my friends out of helping.

Vivian was convinced that Alek would live. That had to be good enough for me.

"Fine," I said into the phone. "I'll get the Sheriff to share her info with you. We'll do the thing. But you'd better deliver, Noah."

"Consider it done," he said. Then he hung up on me, denying me even that small satisfaction. Damn vampires.

I set my phone down and opened the bag of kettle chips, staring into the greasy interior. Then I looked up at my silent, but anxious friends. They all looked ready to expire from curiosity and barely hanging onto their tongues.

"So," I said, trying for casual. "Who wants to go on a quest?"

Everyone crashed at my place that night. Vivian slept on the couch. Harper and Ezee slept in my bed while Junebug and Levi took the guest room. I got a little sleep, most of it dozing off in the chair by Alek's head.

Rachel was surprised when I called her and told her to give everything she had to someone who would be calling. I let Noah know the Sheriff was ready to hand over info and made him swear that he'd call as soon as he knew anything.

Junebug and Vivian were going to stay with Alek, promising to call if he woke up or anything changed. I felt bad about Vivian canceling her appointments, but she assured me that nothing was scheduled that couldn't wait. Rachel still had deputies going by regularly and would keep that up. I don't know what she was telling them, but figured she was used to handling that stuff so I'd let her. It was nice to not have to worry over every detail of every problem. I guess that's what friends are for, right?

Lara was going to run the shop as normal. All the things were ready for us to go.

Harper, Levi, and Ezee, of course, were coming with me. I'd known the moment I told them about what the Archivist wanted that they would. I'd even managed to convince Levi not to go to his shop and get weapons.

"We're looking at an empty house. No guns," I said again around the last mouthful of waffle as we prepared to leave. It was just after dawn, but given how fitfully we'd all slept, we were ready for an early start. It was a long drive ahead.

"This house isn't even on Google Earth," Harper said. "Weird." She was staring at her phone.

"Weird shouldn't surprise anyone," I said. I knelt down by Alek and rubbed his chin. His breathing was strong and steady now, but he hadn't woken up yet.

"He's doing fine," Vivian said with a yawn as she sat up on the couch.

"Call me if he wakes." I stroked Alek's nose, something he normally hated, in the vain hope it would annoy him and wake him. He slept on.

I got up and went to do my morning ritual with the Alpha and Omega and Samir's heartstone. As I walked out of the bedroom with the dagger strapped to my waist, Levi threw up his hands.

"You've got a weapon," he pointed out.

"It tends to follow me around if I leave it places," I said. That was true, but I was also bringing it just in case.

"I'm taking a machete," he muttered.

"There's one in the trunk," Junebug said as she wrapped her arms around him. "Be safe."

We took one of Levi's cars and let him drive, with Harper in front with the map Noah had given me to navigate since our GPS wasn't finding the address. I was more tired than I thought, because I barely remembered most of the drive out to the house. I came awake with a crick in my neck as we pulled onto a long gravel driveway. The land here was quite barren, only scrub trees and lots of rock breaking up the monotony. The house perched up a big, rocky hill, like an Edward Gorey rendition of a manor.

ANNIE BELLET

Noah's information about it was pretty sparse. The house was two stories, with six bedrooms and four bathrooms and done in a Victorian style. Or what some crazy architect imagined was Victorian. There was a round tower portion up front, overlooking the steepest part of the hill, with leaded-glass windows that glimmered in the morning sun and turned blinding as we approached.

"Looks haunted," Harper said.

"Looks like someone's idea of haunted, anyway," Levi said.

"Stop here," I said. I didn't want to park too close. We could walk the last couple hundred feet up the hill.

Levi pulled over, putting the car next to a boulder. We climbed out, stretching limbs and taking a minute to sip out of water bottles and work out the travel kinks. I'd opted for jeans, a plain white teeshirt, and my leather hiking boots that the store clerk had sworn up and down could resist almost anything. I had yet to put that to the test.

I checked my phone. No calls, but no signal out here either. Figured. I decided to leave it in the car. If something bad happened, at least that would be one less thing I could destroy.

Harper, Levi, and Ezee all found they had no signal either and opted to lock their phones into the glove box with mine.

"This is how horror movies happen," Harper pointed out.

"It's just an empty house," I said, peering up the hill. I found myself rubbing my talisman, the gem under my thumb hard and cold, and I made myself stop that. "Remember the rules."

"Stay behind Jade," Ezee said, looking at Harper and Levi with his best "I'm a serious professor and you should listen to me" expression.

"Touch nothing. We know. I'm taking this" Harper took the tire iron out of the truck as Levi retrieved his machete.

"Sure you don't want something?" he asked his twin.

"I'm good," Ezee said, though he seemed less certain now than when he'd said he didn't want a weapon earlier. "That's going to get heavy when you realize you are trying to challenge a house full of antiques to battle."

"Hush, bro. Sorceresses first," Levi said with a mocking bow as he pointed his machete up the hill.

I led the way, letting my magic run through my blood. My skin tingled as we approached and I held up a hand. Concentrating, I felt a weak spell ahead of us. Well, at least Noah hadn't sent us into nothing. A magic user had definitely been here.

I walked forward and looked at the ground in front of the house. The house had a huge wrap-around porch. Just in front of the wide steps leading up to an iron-banded front door, I saw traces of white on the ground.

"Salt," Ezee said, coming up beside me. "That's what it smells like."

"Stay here," I said. I walked parallel to the salt line around the side of the house, picking my way over gravel and occasional larger stones, aware of how loud my footsteps sounded. I heard nothing from inside and felt no more magic. The spell was weak, the circle, if that's what it had been meant to be, ended just around the corner.

"Old circle, I think," I said as I walked back to my friends. That was in keeping with Noah saying the house was empty also. "Not recent magic. I don't think it'll harm us, but let me go first."

"Don't forget to check every square for traps," Harper joked.

I made a face at her, but was secretly relieved my friends were enjoying themselves. I hoped this excursion would be boring, but at least we could have a little fun with it anyway.

I detected no scent or feel of magic on the front door and the key that Noah had included in his folder of stuff fit the lock. It was a disappointingly modern key, like something you could find at any hardware shop.

"Looks good to me, guys," I said, echoing the swan song of every rogue in every game ever. I opened the door.

I almost expected something to jump out and say boo, but nothing did. The door opened into a foyer area that had a built-in bench of dark wood and a coat cupboard. Beyond that it opened up into what looked like a parlor or formal living area to one side and a dining room to the other. Stairs split the hallway ahead, leading up. The sunlight from the uncurtained windows was bright enough to illuminate the house, but I tried a light switch just the same. The hall light came on, revealing a door further down, by the stairs.

The house smelled dusty, with that staleness that comes from being unlived in. Beneath that scent was something I couldn't quite place, a sweet smell. Or maybe a rotting one. I looked back at my companions.

"Smells like a possum died under the porch and nobody noticed," Levi said.

Ezee and Harper nodded, peering past me into the house.

I shrugged and walked inside. There were some paintings on the hallway walls, generic landscape stuff like you'd see in a hotel or restaurant. Whoever had owned this house hadn't had much style. The dining room was empty, no table, just a parquet floor with streaks of dust or dirt across it, like something had been dragged through. With that comforting speculation, I looked into the parlor. Here there were two heavy wood couches upholstered in dark brocade, in keeping with the faux-Victorian exterior. They faced each other over an ornate table inlaid with a peacock. There was a fireplace with a heavy iron grate and two vases, also with birds on them, perched on the mantel.

I felt around with my magic. There was the trace of a spell here, too, but nothing new, and nothing specific to an item. Magic items are the easiest to detect for me. I've had a lot of practice and gotten the feel for them down to nearly a science. I felt no warm hum nor smelled any foreign magic on any of the things my hands lingered over as I moved around the parlor.

There was a set of French doors at the back of the parlor that led to a formal study.

"I like this guy's taste in desks," Ezee said, going to the huge carved wood desk with its marble top that dominated the space. Dark wood bookshelves completed the room, though no books were on them. Ezee didn't touch the desk, but I could tell he wanted to.

No magic in here. No items in here, not even art left on the walls, though I could see tiny holes in the dark paneling where things had hung once upon a time.

"What are we looking for again?" Levi asked.

"Magical items?" Harper said, turning in a slow circle, taking in the empty shelves.

"Anatomy jars," I said. The Archivist had tried to be casual about it, but it was clear what he was really after. Whatever was in that jar or jars, that was what mattered.

"Call me crazy, but this doesn't look like the house of a mad scientist. It looks like someone already looted it or moved out." Ezee turned away from the desk.

"Maybe the kitchen has stuff," I said. I was inclined to agree with him. The salt circle outside was too old for me to tell what it was trying to do, but it bugged me a little. Was it some warlock's crude attempt at a ward? Or was it there to try to keep something in? I kept those thoughts to myself. No point worrying my machete and tire iron toting friends if I didn't have to.

We went back across the hall. Just as I was about to walk into the dining room to see if the kitchen was through the double doors there, Levi caught my arm with his free hand.

"Wait," he said. He bent low and tipped his head to one side. "Those look like drag marks to anyone else?"

"Yeah, I see it now," Harper said.

Well, so much for keeping that disturbing thought to myself. "Maybe from taking the table out?" I said.

"They swipe toward the kitchen or whatever is beyond those doors." Levi motioned with his machete.

"Maybe we should check out the upstairs first?" I said. Being here was playing hell on our nerves, I thought, that's all it was.

The little door in the hallway by the stairs turned out to be one of the bathrooms. It also had nothing in it, though the toilet flushed when Levi leaned in and checked "in case we need it later, that was a long drive." We went up the stairs where there should be, according to the scant information, six bedrooms and three of the four bathrooms.

The bedrooms were utterly bare except a couple more of those ugly paintings on the hallway walls. The dust up here was fairly thick, no suspicious drag marks, no signs of life for months at least.

"I'm starting to get annoyed at that vampire," I muttered as we clomped our way back down the stairs and reconvened in the parlor.

This felt like a wild goose chase and I was worried what that might mean. Had Noah wanted me out of Wylde for some reason? I felt sick to my stomach now leaving Alek behind. The only consolation I had was that Brie, Ciaran, Junebug, Vivian, and Rachel were all watching over him. Even I would think twice about messing with that crew. Maybe Noah had just had bad information, or maybe that spell out front had spooked him for some reason, made him think this place was more than it was.

"To the kitchen?" I asked.

"Let's go," Harper said, hefting her tire iron.

We crossed the dining room without incident and I

was just about to push open the swinging doors when Ezee called out softly, "wait."

I turned, my magic so ready for action that my skin felt like it had lightning running under it, and watched as he went to the other side of the room where something was stuck in between the baseboard and the wall. Ezee tugged it out.

"What do you make of this?" he asked, bringing it to us.

It was a strip of khaki cloth, like a coat or pants might be made from, with a dark stain on it.

"Definitely blood," Levi said, sniffing the cloth. "Old but not that old. A few weeks, at most."

"Stand back," I said. I turned to the doors and kicked them open, one hand going to the dagger at my waist, the other up and ready to blast anything on the other side.

The doors flew backward and hit stoppers to either side, swinging back in toward me. I caught a good look at the kitchen, which had as bare as the rest of the rooms. It was galley-style with dark wood cabinets, pale marble counters, and nothing of interest that I could see in the glance I got. No demons or shifters or even a rabid squirrel.

"Clear," I said, moving forward. I shoved the door back open and walked into the room. The drag marks continued right up to the wall, where they stopped. There was blood, obvious even to my less acute senses, spattered against the wood panel there.

"That's not ominous at all," Harper said, coming in behind me.

No hum of magic here, either. Just a wide drag mark through the thick dust across the deep grey tiles, a little spatter of blood, and nothing.

"That's weird, but," I trailed off with a shrug. "That's the whole house according to the documents Noah gave me. I guess we're done?" I kept staring at the wall panel.

"There's a draft here," Harper said, moving past me and up to where the blood spatter was. "Almost as if..." she pushed on the panel and we all heard a click. With a tiny squeak, the panel yawned open.

"Oh good, Harper found the secret door," Levi said.

We crowded forward to look into the opening. It was dim inside, the light from the kitchen windows failing to penetrate very far, but I saw stone steps leading downward, into darkness. The air coming up from those depths was cold and smelled heavily of decay.

"Hey guys," Harper said as we backed away from that smell and looked at each other. "You remember that game Jade ran about three years ago? The one where we had to go into that haunted keep and found that dungeon underneath it? Remember how the middle corridor had this huge metal door and from behind that door we could hear ominous chanting?"

For a moment I was confused. Then I had to swallow a laugh as I remembered what had happened and realized why she was bringing it up.

"I remember," Ezee said. "We chose the other paths. Then we went back by that door and the chanting was getting louder."

"And you fuckers looked at all your loot, and went right home," I said, grinning.

"Yeah, good times," Levi said. "Why ever do you mention it?"

"Oh, no reason," Harper said, looking pointedly at the gaping stairway which smelled like refrigerated roadkill.

"We don't have any loot yet," I said with a sigh. I wanted nothing more than to get in the car and go home, but a promise was a promise, even to a vampire.

Besides, who were we even kidding? We all knew we

were totally going down those stairs. I channeled my magic into my talisman, making it glow bright blue to illuminate our way. I wanted to draw the Alpha and Omega, but then had a vision of slipping on the stairs and impaling myself, so I resisted that urge.

"Bet you wish you had a weapon now," Levi muttered behind me.

"Shut up, Levi," Ezee said. His tone said his twin had scored a point there.

"Stay a couple steps behind each other," I said. Hoping it was just an unfinished basement, but doubting it, I started down the stairs.

Alek

Alek woke slowly. First he smelled bacon, not strongly, just a lingering trace in the air and mixed heavily with coffee. Then he smelled wolf, his muscles tensing until he identified the scents mingling with the wolf as antiseptic, iodine, neoprene, and lemony soap.

Vivian, he thought, not yet opening his eyes. His body felt heavy, like he'd been asleep a long time and wasn't quite ready to awaken yet. His throat hurt, but not like it had in his last memory.

What he didn't smell was Jade. Her faint scent was there, of course, for he'd realized he was in their apartment already, but he knew she wasn't in the room. The only breathing he heard was the little vet's light breaths close beside him. Eyes still closed, Alek buried the seed of panic growing in his belly and tried to remember exactly what had happened.

Jade had dropped to her knees and he'd started moving forward when he heard the gunshot. He couldn't remember if she was bleeding, there was no time before the white hot pain slammed into his throat, more pressure at first than anything. The feel of his blood spurting through his fingers. He didn't remember falling, but the picture of Jade's face above him swam into his mind. She was telling him something.

Telling him to shift. His last memory was her hands on his and him reaching into the Veil, calling for his Tiger through the pain.

A gun couldn't kill Jade. She'd been conscious enough to help him. Alek relaxed. Jade was fine, just not in the room.

He heard footsteps and caught the smell of cinnamon oil. Junebug.

"Sheriff is on her way over to check on things," Junebug said, presumably to Vivian.

Alek opened his eyes and raised his head slowly, blinking against the bright morning light streaming in.

"Oh my god, you're awake!" Vivian got up from the chair beside him.

"Alek, hey," Junebug said, smiling at him as she walked into the living room.

Alek swallowed. His throat felt like his fur was growing on the inside, but he could breathe fine. He didn't shift yet, unsure what state his weaker human form might be in.

"Get him some water," Vivian said. "Can you drink? I can put another IV in if you want."

That explained the odd feeling in his left foreleg. Alek twisted his head around and saw the thick needle taped there. He went to pull it out with his teeth but Vivian bent down and pushed at his head.

"Stop that," she said. "I'll take it out, here."

Junebug brought over a mixing bowl of water and Alek found himself incredibly thirsty. He lapped up water until he was licking the empty bowl. He raised his head and looked around, trying to communicate who he was looking for. Where the hell was Jade? How long had he been unconscious? He tried to get to his feet but his legs were stiff, the muscles weak and half-asleep from being in the same position for who knew how long.

"Easy," Vivian said, a furrow forming between her brows. "You took a bullet to the neck, do you remember?"

Alek sank back down, flexing muscles to stretch out more slowly. He looked at Vivian and nodded his head. His tail started to flick back and forth on its own and Alek stilled it with effort. It wasn't Vivian's fault he was weak and didn't feel safe shifting to human just yet.

"You almost died. I'm surprised you woke up this quickly. It's been about twenty hours."

Alek looked around in what he hoped was an obvious manner. Then he bumped the couch beside him with his head and stared at its emptiness pointedly before looking back at Vivian and Junebug.

They looked at each other and then the light seemed to go in Junebug's eyes.

"Jade isn't here," she said, stating what Alek already knew. "She had to go do a thing." Another glance at Vivian.

The vampire's request. Jade had left him possibly dying on her floor to go rob a house for a vampire? The growl rumbled in his sore throat before he could suppress it. She'd left him, gone off alone. There was no way Jade would have done that without some kind of pressure from the vampire. He stared intently at Vivian and Junebug.

"She didn't go alone," Junebug said. "She took the twins and Harper with her. She didn't have a choice, Alek. The Archivist didn't leave her a choice from what I could tell."

No, he wouldn't, Alek thought. And Jade had done the intelligent thing for once and chosen not to make yet another powerful enemy by ignoring the vampire's request. His mate was growing up.

The sound of the Sheriff's SUV in the parking lot caught all their attention and Junebug went to open the door as Vivian quickly explained that she, Brie, Ciaran, Junebug, and the Sheriff were all on duty to keep him safe while he healed and until Jade got back that night. Alek smiled inwardly at that. Jade had left him well protected. His initial worries were soothed. She was alive and well enough to go on the vampire's mission, and he had plenty of back-up here in case whoever had shot him decided to try again.

Alek hoped they would try. He didn't know who had shot him, but given what a small place Wylde was, he felt it likely that those two outsider wolves had something to do with it. Their presence in town could be coincidence, but more than forty years of being a Justice had killed most of his belief in coincidences.

Rachel came into the apartment and immediately crossed to where Alek sat, a huge grin splitting her face. For a second Alek thought she might pat his head and his lips slid back from his teeth. Stopping short of doing so, Rachel shoved a few strands of black hair off her sweaty forehead as she took off her cap. She smelled like coffee grounds and gun oil mixed with her musky wolf shifter scent.

"Good to see you awake," she said. "I'm working on some leads with the shooting. That guy Jade had me talk to has all the information as well, so we'll see. Those bastards won't get away with this."

That was Rachel, Alek thought. Right to business. He liked that about her. She wasn't one for platitudes or coddling. They worked well together for that reason. She wasn't awed by his past as a Justice but she didn't underestimate what he was capable of, either.

Her cell phone rang and she held up a hand for silence as she answered.

"Sheriff," she said.

"Got a report of suspicious activity," a man's voice said in the phone, clear to Alek's sensitive ears. "You said you wanted to hear all those personally?"

"Go," Rachel said, looking down at Alek and raising

an eyebrow.

"A Mr. Coleman called in. Says he lives out off Brightcreek. His neighbors are away on vacation but he swears he's heard a car pulling into their driveway at night, and the sound of the garage door opening. Said he walked around and knocked, but everything was locked up and quiet. He's heard about the gunshot false reports from his ex-wife's sister who's dating Teddy at dispatch, so he figured he should say something just in case kids are pranking the house cause they are away." The voice on the phone ran out of breath and stopped their report with a little hiccup noise.

"Any of those false reports recorded in that neighborhood?" Rachel asked.

"Hang on," said the voice. There was the sound of typing, the click of a mouse. Then, "Nope, sorry Sheriff. Nothing out that way. All reports been on the Juniper side mostly except that one downtown yesterday. Should I send someone around to check it out?"

"Nah," Rachel said. Her voice was casual but her expression was tight with speculation. "I'll head out that way on my rounds. It's probably nothing, just a lonely man hearing things in the night."

She hung up and slid her cell into its special pocket

on her utility belt.

"Think it's nothing?" Vivian asked.

"I don't know," Rachel said. "I'm going to swing by though. It's the closest thing to a real lead I've seen, so it can't hurt. That neighborhood is quiet and has houses far apart enough to make a decent hiding place."

Alek growled. The Sheriff was planning on going out there all alone. She was used to working alone, she'd told him as much with a wry grin when he'd started riding along with her. Rachel had made sure if he was working for her, he knew that former Justice or no, he was working *for her* and would obey, more or less.

He couldn't let her go alone, just in case this report wasn't "nothing." Whoever had shot him had known how dangerous he was. Alek would have taken himself out much the same way if he had to. Sniping, if the shooter was very good, was pretty effective against shifters. A high-caliber round to the head would put down most supernatural critters, and the finishing blow could always then be dealt close up if more was needed. Head shots weren't simple to make at any distance, which Alek speculated was why he was still alive.

The shooter had been good, but not quite good enough. Jade had seen something and moved into the shot, necessitating the first shot which had to drop her out of the way. That was a seriously risky move, something done spur of the moment. A truly patient sniper would have waited or slipped away and looked for a better moment. It was a small bit of information, but Alek filed away those thoughts. To fight his enemy, he had to know his enemy. Any information could be useful later.

"Glad you are awake, friend," Rachel said. "I'll swing by after I go look around that house, bring some food for you all if Brie hasn't beaten me to that yet."

"Thanks," Junebug said. "We'll call Jade and let her know Alek is up. Good luck."

No, Alek thought. Rachel was not going alone.

They'd shot him. He was the target. Whatever this was, it was his problem.

He heaved to his feet, stretching his back and barely resisting the urge to unsheathe his claws and dig into Jade's carefully chosen carpet as he did so.

"You aren't coming," Rachel said, glaring at him. They were nearly eye to eye now that he was standing. "You won't fit in the car, for one. For two, you were just shot in the fucking neck yesterday. No."

Alek snorted. She had a point, but it didn't matter. Either his human form was healed enough to put in work, or he wasn't. There was only one way to tell. He reached into the mists at the back of his mind and called to his human self.

His throat didn't feel like it had fur growing it in, it felt like it had knives jammed down it instead. Alek stumbled forward but stayed upright, barely managing not to crash into Rachel as she stood, hands on hips, now glaring up at him.

"I am fine," he said, the words like gravel being vomited out of his throat. The scent of blood swamped his nostrils and he looked down at himself. His chest was covered in dried blood, his clothing caked with it. "A shower, I think."

"Sure," Rachel said. "You go shower." She gave him a tight smile.

"Rachel," he rasped as he moved slowly toward the bathroom.

"Yeah?"

"You leave without me, I will shift, run through the middle of town, and hunt you down. I will tear the tires from your car and turn them into tiger chew toys."

His threats were somewhat empty, since he wouldn't compromise shifters like that, but from the look on Rachel's face—a mix of amusement and doubt—his point had gotten across.

"You're explaining this to Jade," Vivian said with a sigh.

Alek nodded as he walked away. Jade had a favorite saying, something about better to ask forgiveness than permission. It was time to test that saying. He was confident she'd forgive him.

This was his mess. The shooter was after him, had hurt his mate. Alek grinned at himself in the mirror, his teeth white in his bloody face. The shooter would learn that if you shoot a tiger, you'd best not miss.

8

The stairs spiraled down into the darkness, the scent of decaying flesh growing until my eyes watered and the back of my throat stung. I could only imagine how much it must have sucked for my three shifter companions. They all had noses far more sensitive than mine. Nobody said a word as we descended. All of us were straining to see and hear whatever might be lurking in the dark ahead.

The stairs ended after a final turn, opening up into a large chamber. I couldn't see the walls on the far side. In the middle was a faintly glowing object. I moved toward it, one hand on the Alpha and Omega, the other holding my D20 talisman and aiming it like a flashlight.

"There's a switch here," Harper said behind me.

"Don't..." Ezee started to say as I turned around but it was too late.

Harper hit the switch. Lights flickered on around us, strings of cheap Christmas bulbs crisscrossing the room. The chamber was about thirty feet across, with an old-fashioned door in the far wall. The light glinted off its iron bands. The light also shone off the floor, illuminating a circle I'd nearly walked onto without noticing.

The circle was far more complex than the simple salt one outside the house. This one had been inlaid into the stone with copper. The design was intricate and I had no idea what it was supposed to do. Inside the circle was the object I'd seen glowing. It was a smallish crystal jar, like you might keep cookies or candy in. Except it appeared to hold a fist-sized chunk of flesh suspended in phosphorescent liquid.

"That doesn't exactly look like an anatomy jar," Levi said, coming up beside me.

"Where do you think that door goes?" Harper asked.

"That's the epitaph of gamers everywhere," Ezee muttered.

"Don't cross the circle," I said. They all looked at me like I was an idiot for even thinking I had to tell them and I grinned, feeling sheepish.

"There's an altar thing over here," Ezee said, walking around the circle. He pointed to where the stairwell made a natural cubby.

I carefully walked around so I could see from his angle. There was a stone altar carved out of the wall. On it was a katana in a lacquered wooden sheath. No candles or other typical altar accoutrements.

"Think it is safe to touch?" Ezee asked me.

I pulled on my magic and focused. There was magic in the room, which I already knew, but it seemed to focus on the circle. The power there was steady and oddly warm. I thought for a second I could hear a heartbeat but it faded as I let my magic pull back. The smell of dead things did not fade, alas.

"Magic is concentrated in the circle," I said. "It looks good to me, guys."

Ezee gave me a sideways look. That was the line his rogue often uttered when he'd checked for traps and wasn't sure his roll was high enough to matter.

"Don't open that," Levi said behind me.

I turned to see Harper feeling around the door for a

latch. There was only a keyhole as far as I could see, no handle. She pulled out her multi-tool and then produced a bobby pin from her pocket.

"Jade said it was safe," she said. "I'm gonna open it."

"Whoa, I did not say it was safe. I said it wasn't magic."

"This sword is old," Ezee said. He'd moved to the altar and picked up the katana.

I couldn't keep my eye on everyone at once. I'd known bringing them here would mean trouble in the end. Damnit.

"Hey, conference time," I said, walking toward Levi and Harper.

Ezee followed me, holding the sword by the sheath. "I have a weapon now," he said to his twin.

"Unless it's rusty," Levi said. "Or cursed."

"Time out," I said. "That jar is probably what the vampire wants. So let's figure out how to get it, and get out of here? That means not picking that lock, Harper."

Harper was crouched in front of the door. I heard an audible click as she wiggled her tools around.

"Whoops, too late," she said, straightening up. The

door eased open a crack, cool air streaming into the chamber.

"Close that," I said.

Harper leaned against it and the door closed. "Don't think it'll stay without me leaning on it unless I can somehow relock it."

"Where did you learn to do that?" Levi asked.

"My uncle."

"Not rusty. Damn, look at that blade," Ezee said. He'd pulled the sword part way out of the sheath.

The blade was lovely, the metal folded and laminated into a water-like pattern. I couldn't help myself as I bent and looked closely at it. The tsuba had a simple, solid design with a dragon picked out in bright metal on it, perhaps copper or bronze. There was a signature stamp but it was worn and difficult to read.

"Ishimaru?" I guessed, though there was more to it. A name, most likely.

"The samegawa is in good condition," Ezee said as he slid the blade back into its sheath.

"The what?" Levi said.

"The ray skin on the grip, under the cord here. Cord feels like silk, too."

"That's cool and all," I said, looking for focus here.

"But we need that jar and I think my nose is going to stage a rebellion if I have to stand in this stink much longer. How the hell you peeps aren't dying from the smell, I don't know."

"It's a little musty and smells like maybe something died under the proverbial porch, but it isn't so bad," Levi said with a shrug. He clicked his tongue ring against one of his lip rings and looked at his twin, who also shrugged.

I blinked at them. My nose was adjusting a bit to the smell, but not enough to stop me from needing serious mental effort not to gag.

"It's really not that bad," Harper said behind me.

The answer hit me as I looked past Ezee and Levi to the circle with its glowing jar. I wasn't smelling the air, not exactly. I was smelling the magic.

"I think it is the magic," I said aloud. "It smells like rotting corpses. Freshly rotting corpses. Bad enough to make my throat hurt," I added, trying to convey what I was experiencing.

"That's bad, right?" Levi asked.

"I honestly have no idea," I said. "But I don't see how it can be good." I had a bad feeling about this whole endeavor.

"We could just leave," Harper said. She sounded less enthusiastic for the idea than she had at the top of the stairs. "Or see what is through this door."

I studied the circle, hoping its patterns would make sense. It had three rings, with what looked like glyphs carved in between the rings. The glyphs couldn't have been writing, however, since I couldn't make head nor tails of them. This wasn't any sorcery I'd ever encountered. A quick search of Tess's memories didn't help. I wasn't willing to dig into anyone else's memories among the victims in my head just yet. It was unlikely that either the Japanese assassin or the warlock would have a clue. They hadn't been sorcerers.

I wasn't even sure I was dealing with sorcery. It could have been a ritual of some kind. The circle itself and its complexity pointed in that direction. I pulled on my magic again and this time sent it deep, feeling for ley lines like the kind that crisscrossed Wylde in abundance. I'd tapped into a ley line once and no desire to try it again, but I knew intimately what they felt like and could sense them more easily now.

Bingo. Beneath the house and this chamber was the junction of two ley lines. Power thrummed deep in the earth. I wished I'd had time to ask my father about the lines. There was so much I didn't know. I pulled my magic and my thoughts away from the lines. My thumb rubbed over the hard bump of Samir's bloodstone. I imagined he knew answers to some of the questions I had in this moment.

With a shiver, I shoved away that thought. I would not be tempted. Nope.

"You okay?" Ezee asked me, concern in his dark brown eyes.

"Yeah, just feeling around. We're standing on a junction of ley lines. I think that's why this location was chosen by the warlock or whatever he was."

"Was? We sure that he's past tense?" Levi said, waving his non-machete wielding arm around to encompass the chamber.

"Nobody has lived in this house in a while, and nobody stopped us," Harper pointed out.

"Something got dragged around up there," Levi countered, gesturing at the ceiling with his machete.

"But very little blood, and no blood down here," Harper said.

I took a deep breath and regretted it. After the coughing subsided, I wiped my eyes with the sleeve of my teeshirt.

"Let's get that jar and get out of here," I said.

"How are we going to do that without breaking the circle?" Ezee asked, using the sheathed katana to point at the jar.

"Mage hand," I said. "Any chance I can convince you all to go upstairs and wait for me there?"

"Nope."

"Not a chance."

"Nice try though."

The twins moved over to stand against the wall by Harper. She continued leaning on the door, her crowbar at the ready now.

I'd known there was a slim chance they would take me up on the idea, but I'd had to try. I turned away from them and went back to studying the circle. I wanted to leave that damn jar right where it was. Damn my sense of obligation and honor. The lid of the jar was silver, with thin silver bands snaking down the jar and appearing to secure the lid onto the jar by running underneath the bottom. I hoped that meant the jar wouldn't spill easily. I had a feeling that Noah wanted what was in that jar, not just the vessel itself.

My magic hummed in my blood, strong despite its use the day before trying to save Alek. Alek. Damnit. I wished I hadn't even thought about him. Vivian had said he would be fine. I had to believe that. I'd be home in a few hours anyway, provided what I was about to do didn't blow us all up or suck us into some kind of void or whatever might happen if I broke the circle.

Pushing away those super joyous thoughts, I put up a shield in a half circle around us, anchoring from my left hand. Running two spells at once wasn't simple, but these spells weren't flashy, so I was hoping I could manage okay.

If I'd wanted to be really honest with myself, I was a little out of practice compared to where I'd been in the run-up to fighting Samir. But honesty is overrated, right?

The shield up and anchored, I used my right hand to direct a thick tendril of magic, picturing it like a big extension of my own hand. The magic was tinged purple so I could see it easily and know what I was doing. As I focused, the tendril took on the shape of an open hand, mirroring my own. I reached forward, sending the magic hand out over the circle. Nothing exploded. My hand dropped and the magic hand also dropped. I closed my hand, almost able to feel the crystalline jar in my fist as the magic hand closed around it. Keeping my hand closed, I raised my right arm up and pulled it back toward me.

The jar, secure in the magic hand, sailed out of the circle and over to me. My lungs gasped out the breath I hadn't even realized I was holding and I heard similar gasps behind me as my friends started breathing again. I hadn't been the only tense one at least. I set it down on the ground, dropped my shield, and walked the two steps forward to pick it up.

"Nicely done," Ezee said behind me.

The jar was warm to the touch, almost like touching flesh, but definitely some kind of crystal. I picked it up.

That's when the chamber started to shake. A huge chunk of rock smashed down from the ceiling.

"Shit," Levi said.

"Stairs," I said, throwing up my shield again, but above us. This time I did it without the aid of my hands as I clutched the jar.

Another huge piece of the ceiling crashed right at the base of the stairs, blocking off the path upward.

"Nevermind," I yelled as rocks bounced off my hasty shield.

"Through here," Harper called out from behind me as I stumbled backward.

I turned and followed her through the now-gaping doorway. Ezee and Levi were right behind me. The hallway was narrow but lit with electric sconces that flickered but stayed on as we moved at a quick and not entirely cautious pace away from the collapsing chamber.

The shaking stopped after about forty feet down the hall. Just ahead, over Harper's head, I saw that the path branched, the hallway dividing into two halls that veered off at forty-five degree angles of each other. Harper stopped at the junction and turned around.

"Should we go back?" she asked.

"Let me jog back and check the damage," Ezee offered. He was already at the back of the line.

"We shouldn't split the party," Levi said. He clicked his tongue against his lip ring. A new nervous gesture for him, I guessed.

"If I yell, come running," Ezee said.

He turned and jogged back down the hall. I hadn't noticed the hall curving, but it must have because he disappeared from sight. After a tense minute, we heard his footsteps coming back. His face told me everything I needed to know.

"Way too much of the ceiling collapsed. I can't even

tell if there are stairs anymore." He shook his head.

"Well, the air smells not too stale, and there are lights. So, maybe another way out?" Harper said.

"Left or right?" I said, turning to look at the hallways.

The walls and floor were stone, rough-cut from what looked like greyish basalt bedrock. Looking up, the ceiling was about ten feet overhead and also stone. Good thing I wasn't claustrophobic. We were deep underground, from what I could tell.

Harper moved into the right-hand passage and sniffed. Then she backed up and did the same for the left.

"Right," she said. "Air is moving more that way and smells fresher."

"That old roadkill smell is stronger here," Levi said.

My nose was fried from the circle's magic but the death incarnate smell had faded as we moved away from the ritual room. The jar in my hands didn't smell strongly of the magic. I imagined the seal on the lid which was keeping the glowing green liquid in was also containing the magic's scent. Small mercies.

"I vote right," Ezee said.

"Take the jar and then get behind me," I said to Harper. I figured it was safe enough for her to hold.

Whatever picking it up had triggered had been in the ritual room. I thought perhaps a delayed reaction to crossing the circle, but I didn't know for sure.

She made a face, but took the jar and tucked it under her arm so she could keep wielding her crowbar in front of her. I started down the right-hand hallway. The electric sconce lights were spaced farther apart in this direction and the sharp bend in the hall took me by surprise. We turned to the right almost ninety degrees and found another door. It was in the same style as the last door. Old wood with heavy iron bands. The hinges were reddish-brown with rust. It wasn't locked, but instead was barred on this side with a thick beam of wood.

"That looks promising and not at all ominous," Harper said, peering around me.

"Should we go back and try the left hall, or see what is behind door number two?" I asked over my shoulder.

"Maybe it is the way out," Ezee said.

"I vote we open the door," Levi said.

Harper shrugged. "Need help?"

Her hands were full and it was my turn to make a face at her. She grinned.

I gripped the heavy beam and heaved it up out of the iron brackets. Harper moved back so I could drop the beam against the wall a couple steps back. I checked my hands for splinters but found nothing. The stinging in my soft gamer's palms must have been from the weight of the old wood. This door didn't gape open once unbarred.

"Here goes nothing," I muttered as I gripped the brackets like they were handles and pulled.

Turns out, there were zombies behind door number two.

Alek

The bullet had torn through the side of his neck and while the wound was mostly closed up, Alek's throat was still a mess of bruising with an angry red furrow. Washing the blood off revealed that the wound wasn't quite closed, either, clear fluid oozing out from the swollen skin when he moved his head too much. Moving his arms also pulled on his neck skin, something Alek had never really thought about before this moment. He opted for a button up shirt and left his pants and shoes on, not daring to bend much.

Intellectually, Alek knew he wasn't in good shape for a fight. It didn't matter. If Rachel found the shooters before he did, if something happened to her while he was convalescing, he knew he'd never forgive himself.

This was his mess to clean up.

"You hungry?" Rachel said as they pulled away from the apartment. Junebug and Vivian had watched them leave with apprehension on their faces, but didn't try to stop him. They weren't crazy. Rachel had just opened the car door and pushed back the seat all the way so he could get in more easily.

Talking was bad enough, and swallowing water had been painful, partially from just moving his jaw. Alek did not want to contemplate what chewing and swallowing solid food would feel like.

"I'm fine," he said. His belly growled, giving lie to his words and he sighed.

"Really? Because I'm always starving after I have to heal." Rachel gave him a side glance that spoke volumes as she turned onto the main road.

"Swallowing is hard," Alek grudgingly admitted.

"Milkshake it is, then," Rachel said.

The kid behind the window in the McDonald's drive-through peered into the Sheriff's SUV at Alek, eyes widening, but he kept his mouth shut, handing over the milkshake and the large Coke.

"Thank you," Alek said as he took a sip of milkshake. The cold felt good on his throat and the sugar would help his growing headache.

"Sure thing," Rachel said. "Just don't do anything rash if we run into trouble, okay?"

"I never do anything rash," Alek said. He sucked on his straw, keeping his body as still as he could. He'd never noticed how many damn potholes and rough spots the roads in Wylde had. Did not humans pay their taxes for a reason?

The neighborhood the call had come from was out on the edge of the town proper, just before Wylde turned into wilderness and ranches. The houses here sat on large lots, most a quarter to a half an acre, giving the neighborhood a private but still suburban feel. Mr. Coleman's house was a pale green ranch style, a build echoed in the houses around it, including the one across the street. The potential target house was pale blue, but looked much the same; single floor, ranch-style layout. Coleman's house was near the road, while his neighbors' homes were set back farther on their properties. Rachel drove by without stopping and turned up the next side street.

"I'm going to walk back, I don't want the car just sitting there in case someone is around. I want them to think I just drove on by like normal," she explained.

Alek sucked down the last slurp of milkshake and opened his door.

"Alek, stay here, please?" Rachel said.

"No," he said.

Her brown eyes met his icy gaze and she backed down instantly, looking away with an audible huff. Alek suppressed a smile. Dealing with fellow shifters was a relief in many ways over dealing with his mate. Jade did not give two thoughts to body language or aggression and she never backed down if she could help it. Of course, if she were here, she wouldn't be walking cautiously down the street. She'd likely go in, magic blazing.

"Something funny?" Rachel muttered as Alek caught up to her with a single long stride.

He hadn't hidden his smile as well as he'd hoped. Ah well. "Thinking about Jade," he said. His mate solved her problems, and anyone else's that she cared about, with fireballs.

"I'm sure she's fine," Rachel said, misinterpreting his comment. "And will be ready to kill you for putting yourself in danger while injured."

"The birds sing, the sun shines," Alek said. He sniffed the air. None of the smells were out of the ordinary. Fresh-cut grass, dust from the road, day-old dog urine on that mailbox post. "No danger."

"Yet," Rachel said.

They approached the house from the side. No car was in the driveway and the double garage was closed up. There was nothing evident from peering in windows, but Alek caught the faint scent of wolf shifter as he rounded the back. Someone had left a shirt hanging over a deck chair. He smelled it, being careful not to touch it and leave his own trace there. His memory tried to place the scent, but whatever it triggered hung just out of reach.

"Wolf," Rachel said. "Not anyone I recognize."

"Shifters live here?" Alek figured she would have mentioned it, but he asked anyway to be sure.

"Nope," she said with a shake of her head. "Human family."

He'd learned she kept a secret file where she tracked the shifters and other supernaturals that lived or came through Wylde as best she could. It wasn't easy being the Sheriff of this place. Lots of things happened she had to help hide from the humans, and Rachel had dodged her share of Council issues as well. He was not the first Justice to be sent to the town.

Just the last. He pushed the bitter thought away.

"Nobody here, but I bet they'll come back," Rachel said.

"Hide in woods?" Alek said, looking at the yard and gauging how well he could hide his tiger-self there. Not well. The yard was large, but a fence separated it from the house behind, and while there were trees, it was well maintained which meant not great for hiding. He wanted to shift, his human body was tired and hurting. He'd be more useful as a tiger at the moment anyway.

"I got a better idea, come on."

Rachel's better idea was knocking on the door of the house across the street and introducing themselves to Mr. Coleman. He was a stocky human with tanned, age-spotted skin stretched thin like paper over his cheekbones and jaw.

"Sheriff, thanks for taking me seriously. Not sure what's up over there, you know?" Mr. Coleman said in a surprisingly deep voice. He glanced nervously at Alek.

"Sure. You mind if we sit a while in your place? It's probably just someone keeping an eye on the place, but we'll stay out of the sun that way while we see if they come back." Rachel smiled at the man, bringing his attention back to her.

"I was just heading out to see my sister, family dinner and all, but you and your, ah, you can stay long as you like."

The front room was a living room with a couple comfortable overstuffed chairs, an uncomfortable-looking small couch, and a very lived-in recliner. Alek's nose told him the place had once, in its distant past, been home to a male cat who liked to spray. Mr. Coleman showed them where the bathroom was and then Rachel managed to talk him out of the house in a gentle, friendly way that Alek almost envied. People obeyed him, they feared him, often they desired him, but they didn't exactly treat him like their new buddy.

"Mr. Coleman needs to take his trash out," Rachel said as she started moving curtains and arranging chairs so they could see out the front window. It gave them a good view of the house across the street.

Alek took a seat after realizing if he shifted, they could run into space issues in the smaller, somewhat crowded living room. It would also make it more difficult to see out the window while remaining in shadow.

"I can keep watch if you want to shift and rest," Rachel said.

He met her too-perceptive gaze and started to shake his head. That hurt and he stopped immediately, suppressing a wince.

"I'm fine," he said.

Rachel made what he interpreted as a "suit yourself, tough guy" gesture and took a seat on the other edge of the picture window. They sat in quiet for a while and Alek started to think perhaps he shouldn't be so stoic. His neck felt tight and hot, even swallowing saliva hurt now. Sitting quietly, he had nothing to focus on except his own discomfort or worrying about Jade.

At least Jade would be fully healed, and she'd taken her friends with her. Alek had learned in the last couple years not to underestimate the twins or Harper. He'd seen them take on bigger problems than robbing a house. They would keep each other safe. No point worrying, he told himself. There was nothing he could do there.

Here he could do something. If they could catch and kill the people after him before Jade got back, that would be one less danger, one less worry on her plate. One nightmare she wouldn't have to pretend she did not have. Alek could not guard her in her sleep, could not keep her safe from the dream-Samir who made her shake and whimper in the night, but he could try to keep her waking hours safe, uncomplicated. Peaceful.

So much for peace, he thought, feeling the burn of the wound in his throat as it slowly healed.

"You think you will know these guys?" Rachel said, breaking the silence. She pitched her voice low, knowing they had no need to speak loudly and not taking the risk even though they were alone.

Alek did not particularly want to talk about it, or talk at all, but sitting silently worrying and hurting wasn't pleasant either. He sighed.

"I do not know. But with the Council broken, the Justices are finding things are not so good." Which was an understatement, but even with the Council out of commission and eating itself from within, Alek still felt loyalty to its former ideals and was not sure he wanted to divulge its secrets, even to a fellow shifter.

"How so?" Rachel pressed.

Alek thought over what he felt comfortable saying and the Sheriff waited patiently until he spoke.

"There are reports of former Justices being killed," he said finally. He left out that he knew some of them had been killed by former Council members or shifters working in their name. Carlos had kept in touch as best he could after the hellish events they had both barely survived in New Orleans. "Others dropping out of touch, though we were never close exactly. Without the Council to foresee danger, without their added power, there is trouble in places. Hard feelings from those we have dealt with."

Hell, he thought ruefully, his own sister would not speak to him because of what he had had to do when her friend broke their laws.

"Chickens coming home to roost," Rachel said. He saw her nodding out of the corner of his eye.

"That is an American phrase?" Alek asked. He was not sure he had heard that one before.

"Sure. Don't you have something like it?"

"Perhaps. I think we would say što poséješ', to i požnjóš," he said. "As you sow, so you harvest." He was not entirely sure of the translation but it was close enough.

"I know that it's probably super secret business, but…" Rachel trailed off and they sat in silence. A car drove by, a woman with two kids in her back seat. It didn't slow down.

"The Council," Alek said after a while.

"All we know are the rumors, even I haven't been able to track down much real information. Only that one of the Nine was killed." Rachel's voice was tight with nerves.

Alek did not blame her. They were talking about the death of gods in a way. The all-seeing, all-knowing power that had ruled shifter lives with an iron fist for hundreds of years.

That rule was ended. Alek's heart felt like a lump in his chest but he knew he had made his choices, and he knew the end had come without his help. New Orleans had taught him that much, at the least.

Turning his head would hurt too much, so Alek rotated his upper body on the chair to face Rachel. He'd hear a car coming, so he was not that concerned with taking his eyes off the house. Her jaw was set, the muscles twitching under tension, and she did not look over to meet his gaze.

"Another of the Nine killed her," he said. Rachel's head turned and her eyes met his, wide with surprise. "I do not understand it all," he added. "But the Nine were once just shifters like you or I. They were given their powers by the Fates, the power to forsee, to predict. But shifters are mortal and such powers were not really meant for mortals."

He paused, searching her expression for a sign that she was closing down, worried that Rachel would not want to hear her gods had been just men and women. Alek had run into that problem already and was gun shy, as the saying went, about facing it again. The only other shifter he had told this to had tried to kill him, after all.

Rachel's dark eyes were wide with surprise but the slight wrinkle in her brow and the tilt of her chin told him she was listening. Her hands rested on her legs, her ankles crossed was the only sign of defensiveness or closing up.

"So they went crazy?" she said. "And you mean like the Fates from myth kind of Fates?"

That was a more blunt way to state it. Alek took a slow breath. The pain in his throat was easing as the minutes ticked past.

"Yes to both, from what I understand. The Council members are no longer stable, no longer anchored in the now, in reality." He was not sure how to explain it, he barely grasped the concept himself. "All they see are death and threats. What once was potential has become real in their minds."

Rachel was nodding along as he spoke. "I guess if you see lots of probabilities and future events all the time, future crimes and danger; that could drive someone kind of crazy after a few centuries. So we're really on our own?" The last was half statement, half question.

"I think we are," Alek said.

"I'm all for law and order," Rachel said. She managed a semblance of her usual grin and Alek relaxed a little. "But even with the Council, stuff slipped through the cracks a lot. I think we'll manage. Our ancestors managed before the Nine, after all."

Shifters had managed to get themselves hunted down and killed by humans a great deal before the Nine, Alek knew. Entire witch hunts and werewolf legends had spawned because of it. But the sound of another car cut off Alek's need to respond. He rotated back and peered out the edge of the window.

The car was a black SUV and it pulled into the driveway of the house across the street like it belonged there. A man wearing a painter's cap and coveralls jumped out of the passenger side and punched a code into the panel next to the garage. The car drove in after the door had lifted, and the driver got out.

"Bingo," Rachel murmured. "Fit Levi's description, don't they just."

The man who had opened the garage turned and looked around at the street, giving Alek a perfect view of his face.

He didn't realize he was growling until the vibration in his chest made his neck hurt.

"These guys your chickens?" Rachel asked as she popped the snap on her holster. Alek heard the scrape of her gun as she slowly drew it.

"Worse," Alek said. "They're Nazis."

The door came free with a hard tug and hit the wall as I quickly let go and stepped back. A rotting corpse launched itself at my face. Instinct and magic saved me as I threw up a shield and the creature was deflected. It bounced off and slammed into its companion.

The creatures were definitely zombies, for lack of a better word. They looked like something straight out of a horror movie. Flesh hung in festering strips off their bones. Their clothes, which might have been teeshirts and jeans once, were shredded and caked with dried blood and probably other bodily fluids I didn't want to envision. Both corpses appeared to be male. Their fingernails were overgrown into hideous claws and their jaws gnashed open and closed again as though they were stuck with a memory of chewing gum.

I turned shield to flame as Harper exclaimed behind me, "Holy shit" and swept the fire forward in an arc.

Turns out, real life zombies don't like fire any more than video game zombies do. The magical flames caught on their flesh and they started to howl as the fire lit them up like corpse torches.

Backing away from the heat, almost falling into Harper, I realized I'd caught the door on fire. The flames ate the dry wood up as we backed farther down the hallway.

"Maybe left?" I gasped when I could finally feel air on my face instead of heat. The hallway seemed clear though the eerie howling screams had not abated. I put up my shield in front of me again, just in case a burning zombie decided to rush down the hall.

"Uh, Jade," Ezee said in a slow, controlled murmur. "I don't want to alarm anyone, but there's a zombie staring at me from behind us."

Fucktoast on a stick. This wasn't going to be easy.

"What's it doing?" I asked, craning my head around to try to see.

Harper pressed herself back against the wall, facing

the direction of the flaming zombies. She had a white-knuckle grip on her crowbar while holding the jar tight to her side with her other hand. I couldn't see around Levi's broad shoulders or over his Mohawk.

"Hissing?" Ezee said.

"Ok, slowly, we move back toward the fire." I started doing exactly that, edging my way back down the hall, shield up.

Right behind me, my friends did the same. The door was still burning and the zombies in the room beyond were now twitching, smoking corpses. I dashed into the room, pushing them to the sides with a wave of force from my right hand. Fatigue edged my vision in red for a moment. I wasn't exactly being magically economical.

Harper, Ezee, and Levi dashed in behind me and we circled up. The room was about ten by twelve with a dark hallway opening directly across the room. To the left of us was another door. The smoke from the fires I'd started clung to the walls and ceiling and swirled over in the direction of that door.

"I think that door leads somewhere vented," I said. "Look at the smoke."

"Zombie," Ezee said. He had the katana drawn and

its blade shone in the flickering light.

The zombie, another rotting male, lurched into view by the burning door. It hesitated there, as though the fire unnerved it. One of its eyes was missing and its jaw hung grotesquely to one side as though something had smashed it.

"How is that thing making noise?" Harper asked. "It can't breathe, right? I mean, I see its lungs."

"It's a zombie," Levi said as though that explained everything.

"Magic," I said. Magic like I'd never seen before. Who the hell would make zombies?

"Brother," Ezee said.

"Brother?"

"You know what this means?"

Levi nodded. "We have trained our whole lives for this." He raised his machete. "Let's kill a zombie."

Movement caught my eye in the hallway ahead. "Um, guys."

"I hear more," Harper said.

"Both directions," Ezee said.

The zombie just beyond the smoldering door moaned and charged forward. I watched long enough to see Ezee side-step it and swing his blade before I had

ANNIE BELLET

to turn and pay attention to the hallway. The smoke had gathered there, too, and while I saw swirls of movement in it, the electric lights didn't go down that way. I was reluctant to throw more fire without a clear target. I'd been wasteful with my power enough already.

"Harper, get that door open," I told her. At a glance it looked like another locked door similar to the one in the ritual chamber.

"I'll have to put down the jar," she said, moving toward the door.

"Do it, we've got you covered," I said, hoping I wasn't lying. No way was I about to let my friends die to a zombie horde. I'd be the worst gamer friend ever.

A glance told me Ezee had beheaded the zombie. Just like in the movies, that had stopped the corpse from moving.

"We'll take this doorway," Levi told me over his shoulder as he and Ezee fanned out.

"I've got the far hall," I said. I backed up so I could stand near Harper while keeping my eyes on the hallway.

Three more zombies flooded into the room. These were in better shape than the last ones had been. They had features still and more flesh with recognizable clothing. These undead men looked like former military of some kind, wearing khaki fatigues like the bit of cloth we'd found in the kitchen. Deep slash wounds in their chests and bellies told how they might have died. One nearly tripped on its own entrails as it rushed me.

I drew the Alpha and Omega, not wanting to face multiple burning zombies or endanger my friends. The dagger lengthened in my hand, going from knife to sword in a heartbeat. Supposedly the blade could kill anything, living or not.

Time to put it to the test. I lunged to meet the zombie charge. The sword stabbed into the zombie's chest and it had no time to even scream as it turned to dust in a blink. I almost fell forward into the next zombie as the weight on the end of my blade disappeared and I had nothing to stop my momentum anymore.

I twisted and hopped to catch myself, throwing my left arm up to block the zombie's swiping hands. Its nails bit into my unprotected skin, raking me. I smelled the fetid rush of air around it as the zombie crashed past me. I spun, gritting my teeth against the pain, and slashed the zombie across the back. Zombie number two went up in dust.

Zombie three ran right into the backswing of my sword and it, too, was reduced to nothing.

More howls and moans echoed from the hallway as I gasped for breath and looked at the damage to my arm. Deep cuts laced my forearm, but my body's natural healing was already slowing the blood loss. Nothing I could do about it now anyway.

"You okay?" Ezee said, pulling my gaze to him.

He stood over a dead zombie with two more headless corpses around him. Levi had another at his feet whose head he'd more smashed than severed with his machete.

"Flesh wound," I said.

"You're not going to turn into a zombie, are you?" Levi asked with a wild grin. "Because if you need me to kill you, I can't be that friend. Alek would murder us and I'm too pretty to go that way."

"I don't think these are those kind of zombies," I said. Great. Another thing to worry about. I shoved even the thought of that aside. This was magic, not George Romero.

"Thought you were training with a sword?"

"Shut up, Levi," I muttered, turning back toward the hallway. "How's that door coming, furball?"

"Working on it," Harper said around the bobby pin tucked in her mouth.

"I hear more coming," Ezee said.

I summoned my magic, power singing in my blood and pushing the pain back with its siren song. I'd be exhausted later, but fuck it. What was the point of being a sorceress if I didn't do magic? I faced the hallway and thought about how to block it off to buy us more time. If this had been a game, I'd have used a web spell. I could do that. Maybe.

Focusing, I spooled power out of myself, picturing a thick, sticky thread. I drew my hand around in a vaguely crisscrossed pattern over the doorway, anchoring the magic to the stone as best I could. Purple light flickered along the edges of the invisible web, showing me I'd done a decent job. Then I pushed more power into the webbing, visualizing heat and fire. The purple glow intensified, tiny flames limning the web.

Zombies spilled out of the doorway we'd come in as I turned to help Ezee and Levi, hoping my web would hold for a bit if more came from that direction.

"Get back," I said to them. I didn't want to swing the Alpha and Omega and clip a friend. Even a scratch from this blade seemed deadly.

The twins fanned out slightly behind me, taking on the zombies that got past my sword. I didn't have to worry about the heads, I just swung the blade back and forth with both hands in a hacking pattern, trying to hit zombies and not hit myself when the zombies turned to dust.

The sword wasn't heavy, but my arms hurt after about a dozen chops that managed to kill four more zombies. They were coming on faster now, a whole horde of them in various states of decay, as though they'd been made at different times. I was too busy trying not to kill myself to pay much attention to the twins or Harper, but not very many zombies were getting past me since I had moved almost up to the doorway now that the burning door was only a smoldering mess.

"Got it," Harper yelled behind us. Then, "It's clear, just a hall."

"Come on, Jade," Ezee called out.

"They are getting through your webbing," Levi said, just behind me. "Let's go."

I heard a sickening crunching noise as Levi smashed a zombie skull. I dusted another and started backing up. Switching the sword to my right hand, I summoned power, bringing my shield up again and using it to force the zombies back as they spilled through the door. Some stumbled over the corpses of their companions, slowing the others behind them.

We'd killed over a dozen and more were still coming. This wasn't good.

Levi had a hold on the back of my shirt and was pulling me with him. I let him guide me backward, keeping sword and magical shield up. The webbing had failed after lighting a couple zombies on fire as they shoved through it. Two zombies crawled over their dead companions, wreathed in purple flames. They lit the dead on fire as they went and the smoke was getting thicker, more oily by the minute.

Then I was through the door. I tried to pull it closed with magic behind us, but the zombies were too quick. One slammed into me and only the sword kept me from getting bit as I swung it, dusting my attacker.

"The jar?" I gasped out as I swung the Alpha and Omega across the narrow passage to keep the zombies at bay.

"Harper has it," Levi said over my shoulder. His hand was still in my teeshirt. "Keep backing up, I've got you."

The stone passage ended in another small room, this one circular. The zombies were pressing down the corridor but the one in front was only recently dead. It must have had some vestige of intelligence left, for it hung back, out of range of my waving sword.

"There's a ladder," Harper said.

I put my shield up, ignoring the dizzy feeling that swept in with my magic this time, and risked a glance. There was an old iron ladder above us that disappeared into darkness overhead. The bottom of the ladder was about ten feet up. The smoke was being sucked up whatever passage the ladder ascended, giving me hope there was something other than more stone up there.

"Go," I said. "I'll hold them off." The lead zombie slammed into my shield and the force shoved me back a foot, my boots scraping on the stone. I couldn't hold this all day. For my friends, I'd certainly try.

"I'll climb," Ezee said. He sheathed the sword and jumped the ten feet, catching the ladder with one hand and pulling himself up like it was nothing.

Shifters. I braced my feet as the zombie slammed my shield again. I pushed more power into it, visualizing purple fire on the outside. Slam into that, shit-for-brains, I thought.

It did. Howling resumed.

"There's a trap door," Ezee yelled down. His voice echoed a long way. "I see sky," he yelled a few seconds later.

The ladder lit up as though faint light was hitting it, likely sunlight. I hoped.

"Okay, everyone who can't fly should climb," I said though gritted teeth.

"I've got the jar," Harper said. "Sorry about the crowbar." I heard it clatter to the ground.

"I have more," Levi said.

The zombies were shoving against my shield in force now, two of them managing to squish into the passage side by side and push. I put another burst of purple fire into the shield, but their weight still pushed me back another foot. Soon I wouldn't be able to hold the doorway. I was too tired to extend the shield too far from my body. I'm better with offensive magic than defensive.

That gave me an idea. I looked back to make sure everyone was up the ladder. Levi was at the bottom. He'd dropped his machete to cling to the ladder with one hand and was holding the other out for me.

"Come on," he said.

I shook my head as the zombies shoved me back another foot.

"Climb," I said. "I can handle myself."

"What are you going to do?" Levi hesitated, though he pulled his hand back and gripped the next rung.

"Go Khaleesi on these bastards."

Levi climbed.

I waited, pushing hard against the zombies with my magic. I willed the Alpha and Omega down into a dagger again and shoved it into its sheath. It went without a fight. Apparently my bloodthirsty sword preferred the living to the undead.

As soon as I couldn't hear the ring of Levi's shoes on the ladder, I released the shield and threw myself backward toward the ladder. My magic still sang in my blood and I let a little of my dragon out. I couldn't shift, but fire was my best friend thanks to my dragon blood. Fire was easy. It didn't matter that I was hurt or exhausted. Fire and I were like peanut butter and chocolate. We belonged together.

I unleashed the fire as the zombies poured into the room. I let the fire fill me and surround me, flames eating my clothing and spiraling out from my skin. My hair came loose and fanned out around me as the flames grew into a whirlwind. I pushed against the floor, riding the wave of flame and heat up into the tunnel above. Below me, the zombies burned and died a true death. A clawed hand almost snagged my leg as I rose. I kicked it, willing even more power into my maelstrom of flame. On the wave of my own personal rocket blast, I shot free of the tunnel in a gout of flames and chunks of burning flesh as bits of zombie were pulled up with me.

The elation died as I slammed back toward the earth, barely catching myself as I curled and rolled on the rocky ground to the side of the passage.

I lay there, breathing fresh air and enjoying the sunlight for a long moment. Then I sat up, taking stock.

My leather belt had survived, protecting parts of my jeans. The Alpha and Omega were fine, as was its magically enhanced sheath. My hiking books had made it, though the tops of my socks and my laces weren't in good shape. My teeshirt and bra were toast. Not even a scrap remained. My braid ties were toast as well, but my hair was fine, if tangled in a way only a year of patient work with comb-in conditioner would fix.

I looked up as Ezee slammed the trap door on the tunnel.

"That was impressive," Levi said.

"Give her your shirt," Harper said to him and before I could form a word of protest, Levi unbuttoned his shirt and handed it to me.

"Thanks," I said.

I tugged it on, my arms feeling like my bones had been replaced by lead. The shirt was long enough on me to cover most parts, since my underwear was only intact where the thicker part of my jeans had been. Ezee helped me to my feet.

"At least we got the jar?" Harper said.

I looked at the smoking bits of zombie parts littering the area around the trap door.

"Don't think they can climb the ladder," Ezee said.

"What now?" Levi looked at me as I looked about us.

Turning full around, I saw the house. We were about a thousand feet from it. The roof was sagging in the back but otherwise it was hard to tell anything had happened.

"Now we go back to the car and get back to Wylde," I said, testing my feet by taking a couple steps toward the house. I felt weak as a drunk mouse, but I'd make it.

"What about the jar?" Harper held it up.

"I don't know yet," I said, starting toward the house, and the car. "But I have a few choice questions for that damn vampire."

I'd never heard of a minor warlock that could make a zombie horde. The Archivist had some 'splaining to do.

Alek

"Like, World War Two Nazis?" Rachel murmured as they watched the man in the driveway.

"Yes," Alek said. "Three brothers, and their father, part of Hitler's Schutzstaffel. SS-Sonderkommandos, from what they claimed. I had thought it might be them, but Levi said they had no rings. They always wear special rings their father made for them before he died. Cast from gold taken from their victims."

"Charming," Rachel muttered. "Where's the third brother?"

"I killed him, many years ago."

"Why not kill them all?" she asked.

That would have made things simpler later, Alek thought. "They surrendered and claimed they did not know the extent of their Alpha's madness. They told the truth about that, so they and the rest of the pack were allowed to go free. Enough had died to make the point, or so we felt at the time. There was no more danger that the Nine could foresee."

The man across the street looked like he was waiting for something, or someone. Alek was fairly sure that man was the older of the two remaining brothers. If so, his name was Arlo. Frederick was the name of the other.

"He watching for something?" Rachel asked.

Another car, this one a small sedan, drove into view. It pulled into the driveway and four men, none of whom looked familiar to Alek, got out. The driver pulled the vehicle into the garage. Then, with another quick glance all around, the men went into the garage and the door came down.

"Seven of them, two of us," Rachel said. "Want to take odds those other five are shifters?" She rose and eased away from the window.

Alek did the same, staying back in case anyone in the opposite house was looking out.

"Likely more wolves," he said. Wolves almost always ran in packs.

"Freyda wouldn't like this one bit," Rachel said. She holstered her gun as they retreated to the kitchen where they couldn't be observed. "I'll call her."

"No," Alek said. "This is my fight. I will not have anyone else get hurt."

"What are you going to do, cowboy? Go over there and start ripping wolves apart in the middle of the damn afternoon? What if they start shooting? What if a stray bullet hits another house or some kid walking down the street?" Rachel glared up at him, her cell phone in her hand now.

"They will shoot at Freyda, they will shoot at anyone who comes near. It makes no difference. But if I am there, they will not shoot. I will make them shift and fight properly." Alek took a step toward Rachel, straightening up to his full height. Even though it hurt like hell, he rolled his shoulders, pushing his chest out.

"For fuck's sake, Alek," she said. She licked her lips and stepped back, dropping her gaze from his eyes to his chest. "Can you even make them shift? Isn't that a Justice power?"

"It is my power," Alek said. He had not lost the abilities the Council had given to him. He was not sure why, but they were useful still.

"I cannot believe I am even contemplating this." The Sheriff sighed and put her phone away. "How do we get close? This isn't an action movie, I can't just smash my car through their front window while we go in, guns blazing. That's somebody's house. A human somebody, who will expect it to be sans corpses and bullet holes."

"You have cleaned up messes before," Alek pointed out.

"Yeah. I call Freyda. Well, Ulfr before her, but the Alpha is good at this stuff," Rachel said. She paced across the kitchen. "Some days I feel like I'm in the mafia," she added. "Fuck."

"Can they replace a glass door?"

Rachel turned back to him. "What do you have in mind?"

Alek told her his plan, knowing she wouldn't like it.

She did not like it. But, as Alek had also known, she agreed.

Alek slipped out of Coleman's house and shifted to tiger in the back yard. The immediate cessation of pain surprised him with its intensity. He had not realized how much he was hurting until he was not any longer. Alek also realized he was starving, but he shoved that discomfort aside, promising his grumbling, twisting stomach a cow's worth of steaks when he was done.

He hoped—though he was not going to hold his breath—that the wolves with the brothers would stop fighting once he had put down their leaders. If they were true pack, however, they would likely keep fighting. He had no authority from the Council behind him to curtail unnecessary bloodshed. Part of him had known deep down that someday Arlo and Frederick might come for him. Even now, many years later, he recalled the naked hatred in their eyes.

Mercer, the Justice who had helped Alek with the mad Alpha, was one of the Justices who had fallen out of contact with the others. Alek hoped it was for non-lethal reasons. Seeing the brothers here, however, he feared they had gone for Mercer first.

They could not know if he was dead or not, but reinforcements implied they suspected he was not and were preparing for that. The lack of news about someone gunned down might have tipped them off, but perhaps not given how quiet shifter communities tried to keep deaths. They had not come at him like a pack, but like the killers they were.

Alek mused as he crouched in the back yard and waited for the distraction Rachel would soon be providing. If anything surprised him, it was that no Justice had been sent after the brothers before now. They had been cruel bastards before they followed a mad Alpha, and he imagined they would still be that way.

In the end, it did not matter. Their objective was clear. There would be no asking them questions. They had committed the crime of trying to kill him, of hurting someone he loved.

Alek was judge and jury. Soon he would be the executioner.

Rachel's vehicle pulled onto the street and drove right up to the house across the way. Alek heard more than saw this, but he started moving immediately. Her vehicle would block some of the view and he had to get across the road very quickly and around the back of the opposite house.

Rachel got out of the car. She didn't have her gun drawn. The plan was that she would approach the front door as though everything was normal and she was just checking up on things. Alek hadn't liked that part, but Rachel had insisted. She did not believe they would start shooting a sheriff without provocation in broad daylight. The brothers had been cautious and careful, she argued.

She was betting her life on that. Alek was not thrilled, but he could recognize when he had pushed someone enough. Rachel wanted to do her part her way. It was not easy, but he decided to trust her instincts.

She knocked on the door and Alek streaked across the road, flattening himself alongside the garage. There was no window in the garage and only a frosted window on this side of the house toward the back yard.

"Can I help you?" a male voice said as Alek heard a door open.

"Hi, sorry to bother you," Rachel said.

What else she might have said was lost to Alek as he started moving again. He cleared the side of the house and rounded the back. The grass was dry under his paws and he could not quite manage perfect silence, so he opted for speed instead.

His plan was to slam his way through the sliding glass door and then start roaring to make sure all the wolves shifted. Rachel would be forced to shift also, but she could fight just as well as a wolf.

The sliding glass door opened as Alek leapt up onto the deck. The man, not one of the brothers, froze in the doorway, staring at the huge tiger. Alek wasted no time. He charged the man and slammed into him. His teeth closed around the shifter's weak, human neck and crushed it in a rush of warm blood.

He dropped the body and roared, shoving his way into the house. Two men shifted to wolves, guns dropping to the floor as they did so. Alek attacked the larger wolf, a red-furred beast. His huge paw slammed into the wolf's shoulder and he crushed its head in his jaws.

Movement caught his eye and he twisted to meet the attack of the other wolf. This one was smaller, with brown fur and white tipped-ears. This wolf was Frederick, Alek thought. He remembered those ears. The hatred in the wolf's eyes was familiar as well, shining through even in animal form. Frederick snapped his jaws closed where Alek's foreleg had been a moment before. Alek used the weight of his body to slam the wolf to the side, deflecting him. He tried to rear up so he could use both paws to slam the wolf down, but his head hit the ceiling fan and threw him off-balance.

Two more wolves charged into the living room. One shifted to human, revealing he was the older brother Arlo, and went for a fallen gun as Alek batted Frederick aside again. Alek roared, forcing Arlo back to wolf form. He would allow no guns. It would not be that kind of fight.

The confined space made getting to the dodging wolves difficult. The wolf that wasn't the brothers tried to circle around behind, going for a hamstring. Alek caught the wolf's hindquarters in his jaws. Bone crunched beneath his teeth as the dragged the hapless shifter back around and threw him toward the brothers.

The motion of tossing the heavy wolf away brought fresh pain to Alek's neck. He had mostly forgotten his injured human form, but the phantom of the wound still lurked in his tiger self. He was not at full strength and he knew he should be more cautious.

A cry of pain from elsewhere in the house was followed with a crashing noise, like a vase falling. Rachel was fighting in the front. There was no room and no time to get to her. Alek had taken out three, with two more in front of him. He hoped that Rachel could handle two on her own.

The brothers were more cautious than their companions had been, now that the initial rush of battle and surprise was passing. They snarled at Alek, crouching as far from him as they could get. Frederick eyed the open sliding glass door. In his head, Alek dared the brother to go for it. He was far larger than the wolves, his reach greater. Their pack mate was a twitching lump against the far wall, unconscious but not dead. Alek had severed his spine, however. He was out of this fight.

His tail lashing back and forth, smacking into the shoved-aside couch behind him, Alek snarled at the wolves. They were at angles to him. He couldn't charge one without leaving his side open to the other. If they had been normal wolves, he would not have thought twice, daring their jaws to get any good purchase on his thick fur and hide. These were shifters, and experienced fighters. Their jaws were larger, stronger. They would know where to strike to hurt and disable, just as he did.

The older brother shifted to human, holding up his hands in a surrendering gesture, palms out.

"Let's talk," Arlo started to say. His eyes flicked

toward his brother, who began to slide sideways and more into Alek's peripheral vision than his immediate line of sight.

Alek had hoped they would make a mistake. It would make it simpler if he did not get hurt more. He did not want to explain that to Jade as well. She would be mad enough he had gone after the brothers without her.

Arlo's mistake was that he thought he was still dealing with Alek the Justice. A Justice would likely have shifted to speak. Once upon a time, Alek would have. Part of him wanted to. He wanted answers to questions like was Mercer alive.

But the Council of Nine was broken. Alek was a Justice no longer.

And these Nazi bastards had shot his mate.

Alek twisted as he pushed off with his powerful back legs. He sprang at Frederick with a speed that even Arlo could not have predicted, using all his extra power from being an Alpha shifter as well as a tiger. His paws smashed into the smaller wolf. Frederick might have been the size of a small pony, but he felt like a chew toy in Alek's grip as the tiger crushed his spine with massive jaws.

Dropping the wolf the moment he tasted brain and

spinal fluid and felt the body go limp and heavy in his jaws, Alek spun back.

Arlo screamed something unintelligible in German and shifted. He had no time to do more than throw himself at death in the form of Alek's rearing body. Alek's heavy paws battered the wolf, the shifter's jaws finding purchase on a tiger foreleg for only a moment before ripping away. Alek barely felt the sting of the wound as he dropped his weight down, pinning the wolf. He racked with his back paws, blood and fur flying in the air around him.

The wolf stopped moving and Alek swiped at the corpse, shoving it aside. A black furred wolf bounded into the living room from the front of the house and shifted. Rachel.

"Had to kill the two back there." She looked around and shook her head. "They weren't going to go down easy, I suppose. I think that one is still alive?"

Alek turned his head. He had not heard the injured wolf's breathing over his own and Rachel's panting breaths. The wolf he had crippled lay in a heap, its chest still rising and falling in sharp, uneven breaths. If the wolf woke up and shifted to human, he might have a chance to survive.

A Justice might have let him live. Alek had let these brothers live once, however. That decision had nearly killed him.

He went to the wolf and rolled him over with his paw. The killing blow was easy and quick, his jaws crushing the back of the neck. When it was done, he shifted to human.

The pain in his throat was almost gone, but Alek knew that was likely from adrenaline and battle high. He would pay for this later.

"It is done then," he said.

"Remind me never to piss you off," Rachel said with a nervous laugh.

"Never piss me off," Alek said. His gaze must have been colder than intended because she licked her lips and took a step back.

"No shots fired, at least. Try to walk out of here without tracking blood around. I'll get clean-up out here." Rachel pulled out her phone and looked around the living room again.

Furniture was shoved aside. The ceiling fan was cracked and half-hanging from its mooring. Blood, offal, fur, and dead wolves decorated the ground. Half in and half out of the sliding glass door, the single human corpse lay twisted, his head almost severed.

"Freyda is going to kill me," Rachel said with a sigh as she hit Send.

Jade is going to kill me, Alek thought. She would forgive him. And now there was no more problem here. No more snipers.

As he had sown, so he had reaped.

The first two hours in the car on the way home, I crashed hard in the back seat, drooling on Harper's lap. I woke up when Levi stopped for gas and sodas. A cold Mountain Dew later, I felt sort of alive again. I checked my phone, remembering they had promised to call if Alek woke up. There was a message from Junebug saying he had and was doing fine. My companions, eavesdropping on the message with their shifter hearing, cheered. With a feeling of profound relief, I had Harper hand the jar over to me.

It was locked via a dial on the top that looked like a combination lock, except it pointed at glyphs that were similar to the ones in the ritual room circle. The silver bands would, I guessed, unlatch if the dial were turned the right way. I had no idea what the right way was and I wasn't about to experiment in a moving vehicle, so I left it alone.

"Looks like a human heart," Harper said. She leaned so far across the seat that her head was nearly on my shoulder.

"Maybe," I said, peering into the phosphorescent liquid. I was tempted to shake the thing like a snow globe but managed to resist the urge.

"Sorcerer?" Ezee asked from the front seat where he had also twisted around to get a look at what I was holding.

I knew what he meant. Was the heart a sorcerer's heart. Trouble was, I had no idea. Seemed possible. The one heart I'd taken from a sorcerer in actual human heart form—present blood droplet gem in necklace notwithstanding—had stayed beating.

"Maybe," I repeated. Question was, whose heart was it if so and did I let them regenerate or whatever would happen so I could ask? Or did I hand it over to Noah Grey like I had promised?

"Necromancer?" Ezee said. It was half question, half statement.

"Could explain why the Archivist wanted me to go get it, being undead himself." I'd been trying not to think about that word, either. But who else raises people from the dead and protects their home with a zombie horde?

If this was the necromancer though, who had put his heart in a jar?

Levi said aloud exactly what I had just thought and all of us were silent as the landscape outside the car grew more forested. Trees blurred by. We were almost home.

"So, if you ate that, we'd know who it was, right?" Harper said as we turned off the highway and toward town.

"I am not going to eat a heart in a glowing green jar that I picked up in a zombie-infested dungeon." I made a face at her.

"It seemed less crazy in my head," she said, unrepentant.

"Also it would kill him or her," Ezee pointed out.

"If it even is a sorcerer's heart," I added.

Without knowing, I wasn't about to chomp down. I likely had until nightfall to figure it out. I tapped the jar like a kid would a goldfish tank, silently wishing we'd left it where it sat. I had to hand it over. Noah had promised to find the men who shot Alek. I couldn't welch on my side of the bargain even if I wanted to.

I would hand over the jar, get the information I needed to protect Alek, and try to go on with my life pretending that the mystery of this heart and all that necromantic magic back at the weird house with its subterranean levels did not bug me one bit. 'Cause I'm a pro at ignoring unsolved mysteries.

Well, I thought, I guess everyone has to do some growing up sooner or later. Maybe this was me, growing up.

It was still sunny and warm when we arrived back at my shop. I practically ran up the stairs, jar in hands. I dropped it onto the kitchen table and went straight to where Alek sat on the floor in tiger form. He shifted as I reached him and caught me in his arms.

His skin was even paler than normal and he was still in some pain, evidenced by the tight line of his jaw and the slight wrinkle in his forehead. His neck was a mess of ridged skin where the bullet had torn through the side, but it was healing. The wound was mostly closed and the skin was pink instead of angry red. He'd cleaned himself up and was wearing a different shirt, though his pants were still covered in dried blood.

"Hey you," I said as I jammed my face against his chest. I hadn't realized how scared I'd been for him until I felt his arms around me. I had secretly feared that I would never feel his warmth, his strength holding me ever again.

"I am here," he murmured into my hair. "What did you burn? You smell like fire and rotting meat."

I looked up at his expression and grinned. "Sorry," I said. "I had to fry some zombies."

"Zombies?" Junebug said as she got up off the couch. "Why are you wearing Levi's shirt?"

"Chivalry ain't dead," Levi said as he crossed to her. "Besides, who would you rather see without a shirt? Right?"

"Modesty is very dead," Harper added. "Dibs on second shower."

"Wait, who gets first shower?" Levi asked as he wrapped an arm around his wife's shoulder.

"Me," I said. "Though there are two showers. I'm using mine. I'll try to leave some hot water."

"I am glad you are safe," Alek said as he followed me into the bedroom. I stripped off Levi's shirt and what remained of my clothing.

"My shoes held up," I said as I tugged them off, pulling out the charred laces. "I'll call and leave a message for the Archivist. See if he has any info yet on who shot you."

The sooner that got settled the better, in my mind.

"That has been taken care of," Alek said as I walked naked into the bathroom.

I stopped and turned slowly around.

"Taken care of?"

"The men who shot me are no longer an issue," Alek said. He had a very sheepish smile on his face.

Alek... looking apologetic. I figured the devil was having an ice-carving competition right about now.

"I'm exhausted," I said. "How about you explain to me in really small words what you mean by that?"

"They are dead." Alek tried to give one of his Gallic shrugs but it ended in a wince, ruining the effect.

"Don't fuck with me right now. Who killed them? Who even was 'them' that we're speaking about?" I folded my arms over my breasts. It's ridiculously hard to feel intimidating when you are naked.

"Shower, Jade," he said. "I will explain after."

"Nope, you're coming in with me and you will explain during."

Alek grinned, wincing again. Moving his head at all clearly still hurt him.

"I can agree to this," he said as he followed me into the bathroom.

I turned on the water to scalding and stepped in as soon as it ran hot. I left the shower curtain open a bit so I could see Alek where he took up a spot leaning against the vanity.

"Start talking," I said as the hot water rinsed away the smell of roadkill, fire, and necromancy.

He talked. I listened until I couldn't help myself anymore.

"Wait, what do you mean, Nazis?"

"Wait," Ezee said as we gathered around the table and the pizza that had arrived, courtesy of Junebug's quick thinking, while we all cleaned up. "What do you mean, Nazis?"

"Former," Alek said. He wasn't eating. Instead he

sipped a large cup of ginger ale, looking miserable. Swallowing, he'd explained, still hurt. Alek slowly told the story again, sketching out the details.

"Kinda surprised Jade didn't kill you for going and doing that on your own." Levi grabbed another slice of pepperoni and pineapple pizza.

"The Sheriff helped," Alek said.

"The night is still young," I said, glaring at Alek. I understood why he had done what he'd done but that didn't mean I was thrilled about it.

Part of me could admit I was sad because I hadn't been there to kill them myself. Part of me was secretly relieved it was done.

"It's still day time. You going to call the Archivist?" Ezee asked.

I swallowed the bite of pizza I'd just taken and looked over to where we'd moved the heart in a jar to the kitchen counter. The jar sat there, innocuous and yet ominous. The smell of necromantic magic had all but faded from it.

If that was a sorcerer in there, could I really turn it over to the Archivist without knowing who it was or what they might have done to deserve this fate? I had no idea what the vampire would do with such a thing.

Sell it to the highest bidder, perhaps. What if some sorcerer bought it with the purpose of eating it and gaining its unknown power? There was nothing healthy-feeling about the necromantic magic we had encountered down below the house out there. It was possible all the things we had encountered were protections put in place by the owner of this heart.

Too many things didn't add up. The drag marks and the scrap of fabric we had found in the house. The varying ages of decay evident in the zombies. The newer ones dressed like soldiers versus the older ones in jeans and the like.

"I don't know," I said, realizing I'd been quiet a little too long. "I mean, I will call him. I might not hand that over though."

"I wouldn't," Harper said at the same time as Ezee said, "I would."

I held up a hand before they could start arguing. I knew the look on Harper's face well when she was ready to defend her position and Ezee had drawn himself upright with his "professor" face on.

"Not a democracy," I said. "This is my problem, I'll handle it."

"You going to pull that lone hero bullshit on us

again?" Ezee said. It must have been difficult to look authoritative and disapproving while brandishing a slice of pizza, but Ezee managed better than most.

"No," I said. I laid out the rough sketch of my thoughts, then added, "So until I know what that heart is, I can't really give it over in good conscience."

My friends were nodding. I felt the weight of Alek's gaze but didn't turn my head to see what his expression was. He had no right to judge me at the moment anyway.

"How will you find out?" Junebug asked.

I pinched the bridge of my nose between my fingers. "Not sure. Maybe see if the memories in my head know anything about it."

"Samir never encountered anything like this?" Ezee asked.

"Dude, not cool. Too soon?" Levi said as I jerked upright, dropping my hand to my D20.

They had misread my gesture as PTSD or something. I felt relief as I realized that.

"It's okay. I just don't know what I'm going to do yet. I'm tired. Let me handle the vampire. Go home, get some sleep, okay?" I was bone weary. Tired of lies. Tired of fighting and mysteries and death.

Everyone ate quickly after that, nobody arguing anymore.

"How do you kill something already dead?" Alek asked, breaking the tense silence. "Just in case," he added as I turned my head and raised an eyebrow at him.

"Cutting their heads off seemed to work," Ezee said. "My vorpal blade went snicker-snack."

"Most things die if you destroy the head," I said.

"You wouldn't," Harper pointed out.

"What would happen if someone cut your head off?"

"Levi!" Junebug shot an appalled look at her husband and reached over to tug on the plug in his earlobe.

"No idea," I said. "And no, I don't want to experiment and find out. Ever."

"But would you regenerate? Would your head grow a new body or would your body grow a new head?"

"Levi," Alek growled.

"Shit, now I'm curious," I said, setting down my half-eaten slice.

"Jade." Alek glared at me.

"Not that we'll find out. Ever. I promise." I made an X over my heart, which immediately felt ironic, given my heart was the one semi-vulnerable organ in my body.

After everyone ate, I shooed them all out with promises to meet up tomorrow, and collapsed on the couch. My cell phone rang. Blocked number.

With a sigh I answered, trying to ignore the sudden pounding of my heart.

"Jade," the Archivist said.

"Kinda early to be up, ain't it?" I said by way of greeting.

"You are back," he said.

It wasn't a question. Did he have someone watching the building? If so, had they seen us come up the steps with the jar? I was wading into shark-infested waters, for sure.

That was the moment when I knew I wasn't handing over the jar.

My heart in my throat, I licked my lips and said, "yes, barely. You failed to mention zombies, Noah."

Silence on the other end.

"Did you find anything else?" he said as though I hadn't just said zombies out loud like a non-crazy person.

"Ritual circle of some kind," I said. I felt it best to

stick as close to the truth as possible. "But I was fighting for my life against zombies. Did I mention there were a fuck ton of zombies?"

"What happened to the house?"

"I torched the zombies. I'm fine, by the way, just some claw marks, nothing serious. The house got damaged when the stairs to the zombie infested catacombs below the place collapsed."

Alek settled down onto the couch beside me and rubbed my thigh. I immediately felt calmer. I squinted at him, wondering if he was working some kind of weird shifter magic on me. Maybe it was just cat magic.

"But you found nothing?" The Archivist's voice had a touch of impatience to it.

"Besides zombies? Nope," I said, hoping I didn't sound too flippant. I was glad we were doing this over the phone. I imagined lying to him in person would be ten times as difficult. "The good news is, the Sheriff took care of the shooters, so we don't need your resources for that anymore."

More silence followed that statement.

"Very well," he said.

"I don't know if those zombies have another way out," I said. I didn't like the thought of them out there, even if they were miles from anywhere.

"I will handle the house," Noah said.

"And the warlock?" I didn't say necromancer, but I was tempted.

"I took care of that."

"Good. We're done then. Even." I resisted the urge to cross my fingers like I was ten again.

"Perhaps," the Archivist said. Then he hung up on me.

"I don't know if I fooled him," I said after I made sure the phone call was over by mashing the power button until my phone turned off entirely.

"We shall see," Alek said, wrapping an arm around my shoulders.

"I feel like I could sleep for a week," I murmured. I was done with necromancers and vampires for the night. Tomorrow I'd go poke Brie and Ciaran and see if they knew anything.

My bed was calling and it sounded damn good. I looked over at the jar. I had no idea what to do with it. I got up and went over to the fridge. There was room in there.

"You are putting that in here?" Alek said from right behind me as I slid the jar onto the middle shelf.

"It's kind of hidden this way," I said. I tucked a container of wilting spinach and a chunk of parmesan cheese in front of it. I doubted being refrigerated would hurt it if it were a sorcerer's heart. "Come on, let's get some more sleep."

I grilled him more on his fight against the wolves before I let him sleep. He'd done exactly what I would have done in his position, so it was hard to stay mad at him about putting himself in danger when he was injured. I was exhausted but it took a while to drift off. I didn't want to see Samir in my dreams. Not after a day of so much death. I finally slept and Samir was waiting, warnings on his lips.

It was almost a relief to awaken as my wards went off like a three-alarm fire in my head.

Alek was up as soon as I slid off the bed. The clock said it was just after one in the morning. I grabbed the Alpha and Omega from the nightstand and buckled the sheath around my hips. I'd gone to sleep in nothing but a teeshirt so I pulled on a pair of sweat pants as I listened for a sign of what had made my wards go nuts.

The magical warning system was still ringing in my head and I shut it down. I wasn't good enough at wards to make them super specific, so now that I was awake, there was little point to being distracted by the hum in my brain.

"Something moving outside," Alek murmured, his voice a graveled growl in the near-darkness. He'd crept to the window and nudged the blinds aside.

I heard glass break below us. Damnit. Whoever was down there was inside my shop now.

"I just finished building," I muttered.

We slipped out of the bedroom toward the front door. There was a deck off the guest room that had a door out to it as well, in case we required a second exit. I peered out the window overlooking the back parking lot.

An elongated shadow moved beneath one of the floodlights in the lot. It looked vaguely human but with greyish skin pulled tight over too-long bones. Glowing red eyes stared straight up at me and its wide mouth opened, revealing a double row of sharp teeth. A demon of some sort, perhaps. Or a ghoul. My mind fixated on that. More necromancy bullshit.

I heard a crash from the shop beneath us. My guess was one of those things was inside the shop, upstairs in the computer room. Right beneath the kitchen where we were standing. The whole apartment shook as something slammed into the floor from below.

"We can't fight these things properly here," I said to Alek, backing away from the window. I yanked open the fridge and pulled the jar out, dumping spinach onto the floor. I'd clean it up later, if we got a later.

"They will follow?" Alek asked as he gathered a gun from the cabinet in the living room.

"Hope so. I'll head to the park by the church," I said, thinking quickly about where I could get to open ground and not endanger anyone when I opened a can of sorceress whup-ass on these things.

Clutching the jar under my arm, I threw open the front door. Magic sang in my blood as I sprang into the air, shoving myself along the ground twenty feet below in a gliding leap. Flying was scary, I preferred a gliding run. It was faster, more controlled, and I got to feel like a character out of Naruto or in a Wuxia film. I touched down briefly in the parking lot, the pavement rough under my feet.

"Come and get some," I said to the ghoulish creature as I leapt forward, racing away from it in another swift gliding leap.

I heard more than saw it follow and narrowly missed being mauled by another of the ghouls as it shot from the darkness toward my side. My glide was too fast for it as I pushed more and more magic against the ground, building speed as I shot down the road toward the park. They were taking the bait.

Trees sped toward me and I had to roll to one side as I nearly clipped a picnic table, reaching the park with far more speed than I'd planned. There were a scattering of lights hung in the trees around that cast eerie shadows but were enough to see by. I dropped the jar into the grass beneath me and drew the Alpha and Omega.

The dagger turned to a sword, the runes and letters on the blade glowing with blue fire. I swung as the first ghoul came at me. It was lithe and fast, and strong as fuck. The ghoul dodged out of the way of the blade and a long-clawed hand swiped at my thigh. The claws met mostly sweatpant, but the tips gouged into my flesh. I stumbled back and the ghoul went for the jar.

Blue fire arced out from my sword as I threw magic into it without a clear thought beyond "No." The ghoul screamed and retreated into the shadows leaving only acrid smoke behind.

I regained my footing and stood over the jar. Where the hell was Alek? These things were too fast for me. I had hoped to end them quickly with the power of the sword, but they weren't mindless zombies running straight into my blade. These creatures had thoughts in their heads and a sense of self-preservation.

The ghoul had come right in for the jar, however. They had a goal that I could potentially exploit.

Deliberately, keeping the moving shadows in my vision as the two ghouls circled me, I backed away from the jar. I pushed magic into a shield around the jar, careful to keep my mental vision of the shield as clear and invisible as possible. I wanted to tempt them into closer range, not hand over the jar by accident.

"Come and get it," I said aloud. I split my magic, holding the shield tight with my left fist as I sent power down into the ground, visualizing the magic tunneling under the grass in a heavy rope.

A heavy, flammable rope.

I'd been right about them being focused but not entirely intelligent. Both ghouls took the bait, charging toward the jar from either side of me. I waited until they were close enough I could smell the rotting magic miasma streaming off their grey, shiny skin.

Then I lit the rope of magic with another focused thought and yanked upward with my right hand, swinging my arm like I held a lasso instead of a sword. A wreath of flame tore loose from the soil, chunks of grass catching fire as the loop closed on the ghouls.

They screamed as magic fire wrapped around them

like a noose. I charged forward, slashing at the nearest one. It tried to dodge but was too slow. The Alpha and Omega sliced a shallow cut across its cavernous ribs.

A cut was all that was needed. The blade's magic burned into the ghoul. It fell back screaming like a dying rabbit on the grass as blue fire burned away its flesh.

Not the effect I'd thought the sword would have, but there was no time to ponder its different reactions to different creatures. The second ghoul had shaken free of the flames and was scrabbling desperately at my shield bubble, trying to get to the jar. It had enough sense of self-preservation to turn on me as I lunged for it. I slammed my left fist upward and across my body, bringing the shield like a physical thing up off the ground and into its side, knocking the ghoul off balance. The Alpha and Omega sliced into its chest like a hot knife through butter, the blue flames so intense now I had to immediately back off as the ghoul fell.

That's when the third ghoul slammed into me from behind, throwing me a dozen feet over the ground. The sword flew from my hand as I tried to tuck and roll. This ghoul didn't waste time going for the jar but followed me as I struggled to my feet and brought fire to bear in both hands.

It was bigger than the other two, with the same elongated limbs, shiny grey skin stretched over a gaunt skeleton, and a truly disgusting double row of teeth. The ghoul hissed at me.

"You need Listerine, buddy," I said through gritted teeth as I regained control of my magic and threw fire at it.

The ghoul charged straight through my fire as though it didn't care about being burned and smashed into me again. Those hideous teeth closed on my left arm as I tried to twist and defend myself. I felt bone crunch.

The ghoul was ripped free of my body by a white blur. I fell backward onto my ass, trying to summon more fire through the blinding pain. Tiger-Alek slammed the ghoul into the ground and raked it with his powerful back legs. Pieces of grey flesh flew, black ichor spattering me, cold as ice hitting my skin.

"It's dead," I said as the ghoul's head bounced away across the grass.

Tiger-Alek snarled at me, his tail twitching as he turned away and stalked in a circle.

"More of them?" I asked.

Tiger-Alek couldn't answer, of course. He moved in

a widening circle around me as I forced myself to my feet.

A glint caught my eye. The Alpha and Omega was about ten feet to my left. The jar was glowing about fifteen feet in front of me.

Sword first, then jar, I decided. Holding my broken arm to my side, I staggered toward the sword. That thing was way too dangerous to leave in the grass. Nausea washed over me as I felt bone chips and edges sliding back into place, pulled by my natural healing magic. It had been a while since I'd broken a bone. Now I remembered why I hated it so much.

I reached the sword and picked it up carefully by the grip.

Tiger-Alek growled and kept growling as circled back toward me, his eyes on the jar.

I started toward the jar and stopped. A humanoid shape detached itself from the shadows. I couldn't make out many features, but it wasn't elongated or proportioned like the ghouls had been. Its eyes weren't glowing, either.

A voice whispered across the distance as it moved with a cautious gait. For a heartbeat I wasn't sure it was even human speech, but then the word made sense.

Japanese. Someone saying "please" over and over until the words ran together into nonsense.

Tiger-Alek crouched, ready to spring.

The shape came into the light, mere feet now from the jar. It had been a man once, of that I was certain. It still wore pants, old fashioned trousers with a line of buttons down the fly. There were dull boots on its feet. Its skin was darker grey than the ghouls had been. There was a gaping wound in its chest where its heart should have been. Raw white edges of rib bone stood out against the ripped flesh, but the creature did not bleed.

The nauseating rotten scent of the necromantic magic swirled around the creature in an almost tangible cloud. I gripped the sword.

Then its eyes met mine as it stopped its litany. Dark eyes. Human eyes. Full of a grief and hunger that punched me right in my own heart.

"Wait," I said to Alek.

He snarled but stayed crouched at my side.

The power of that grief, that desperation, held me back as the creature reached for the jar. Instinct was at war with emotion in my head. I couldn't let it have the jar I'd fought so hard for, but yet…

In that jar was a heart.

This creature was missing its heart.

So I stood, frozen, and watched as the creature turned the dial and the bands on the sides of the jar sprang open like a vise coming undone. The creature dumped the phosphorescent liquid out. It smoked like acid as it hit the ground, some splashing the creature's boots and sending up puffs of glowing green smoke. Uncaring, the creature took the beating heart and pressed it into its chest.

Bones cracked into place and flesh flowed over the wound like a cloth rippling and settling on a table. Color radiated over the creature's skin from its chest, warm golden brown returning to the grey pallor. The creature raised its head, its face no longer as gaunt and its eyes fully human. The eye-watering stench of necromantic magic dissipated as though blown away by a fresh breeze even though the night air hardly moved.

He bowed from the waist and then smiled as he straightened up, revealing even, white teeth with long, sharp incisors.

"Thank you," the vampire said in English. "Where is my sword?"

I kept the Alpha and Omega up in front of me as the vampire walked closer. It took my pain-addled brain a second to realize what sword he meant. Japanese vampire, katana. Made sense in a culturally consistent sort of way.

"Who are you?" I said as tiger-Alek snarled.

The vampire stopped moving toward us, taking the hint from the twelve-foot tiger crouched at my side.

"I suppose you are owed as much for freeing me," the vampire said with a slight incline of his head. He was better with facial expression than Noah. His smile looked almost natural.

"You were trapped?" I asked, noticing he hadn't

answered my first question. We'd get back to that, I decided.

"Enslaved," he said, his lips peeling back from his teeth.

"By the necromancer?" I was half-guessing that part, trying to fill in gaps, wondering just how far down the Archivist's lies went.

"Yes." The vampire stood, arms at his side, watching me with an inscrutable dark gaze.

"Even after he died?" Another guess, based on what I'd been told.

The vampire tipped his head to the side. It was a gesture I'd seen Noah make as well. I wondered if they'd learned human in the same 101 class.

"Who told you the necromancer was dead?"

"I'm asking the questions here," I said, sounding more peevish than in control even to myself.

"Very well. The necromancer is not dead. He is hiding in his lair, to anticipate your next question."

"And you are?" I tried again.

"Ishimaru." The vampire bowed again, though not as deeply as he had the first time.

The name rang a bell in my head and I saw the stamp on the katana in my memory.

"Your sword," I murmured, putting it together. "I thought the maker put their mark on the sword, not the owner?"

I had a dead Japanese assassin's memories living in my head, but he was locked away behind the silver circle in my brain that helped keep me from going nuts with too many ghosts. I had been inside Haruki's memories multiple times, but he hadn't had any particular knowledge of swords that I'd mined for information at least. I had eaten his heart and appropriated some of his magical knowledge, but I wasn't comfortable with reliving someone else's life if I didn't have to.

"I made the sword," Ishimaru said. "Suishinshi Masahide taught me himself." It was clear from his tone that he had great pride in this.

Made me wish I knew more about swords in Japan, and I filed away the name to look up. Standing in a park in the middle of the night with a broken arm was not the time for a trip down vampire memory lane.

"How did the necromancer enslave you?" Back to important things.

"Magic," Ishimaru said. "He has great power over the dead, though you have killed many of his creations. I imagine he panics now." The vampire's lips stretched in a grin. Envisioning the suffering of his former master clearly made Ishimaru happy.

"Will he come after me?" I asked.

I was sick of undead. I prayed my shop hadn't taken too much damage. I had sunk a lot of money into that place already. Plus if Lara saw it a mess and I had to explain ghouls to her, she might think twice about working there, no matter how she'd kept her cool.

"I do not know," Ishimaru said. "I want my sword. Then this is not my trouble any longer."

"I give you the sword, you'll leave here without hurting anyone and never come back?"

He nodded. "I will leave. Answer me this, please. Who told you the necromancer was dead?"

My head hurt, my arm was a mess of twitches and aches, and my right hand was getting tired of holding onto the sword. I willed it down to a dagger and slipped it into its sheath, the action buying me a few precious moments to think about my answer.

My answer was that I was too damn tired to play vampire word games.

"The Archivist," I said, hoping he would know who that was. I had no clue how long he'd been heartless and enslaved.

Ishimaru jerked upright, the muscles in his bare chest and arms flexing. It was the first involuntary gesture I'd ever seen from a vampire.

"He lied," he said in a way that could have won Understatement of the Century if such an award had existed. Then his eyes narrowed and he shook his head slowly. "He sent you for the vessel?"

"Yes," I said. "I kind of didn't give it to him. You're welcome, I'm guessing?"

"We are very territorial," Ishimaru acknowledged. "He would have freed me through true death."

I sighed. I would deal with Noah later if I had to. Hopefully he was gone from here and would stay that way.

"My sword?" Ishimaru said.

"I don't have a phone on me," I said. I was torn. I wasn't particularly keen on standing in the park all night. My feet were growing cold in the grass and post-battle adrenaline dump plus injury was starting to take its toll.

Alek shifted and pulled his phone out of his pocket. He didn't take his eyes off the vampire.

"Ezee," I said.

Alek called our friend. "Bring the sword to the park

by the church," he said after I heard the murmur of Ezee's voice in the phone.

Ezee must have asked what was going on, though I couldn't make out the words.

"The owner would like it back," Alek answered. "No. Yes. Good." He hung up. "Twenty minutes," he added before shifting back to a tiger.

"I'm going to go sit at that picnic table," I said, not entirely sure if I was talking to Alek or Ishimaru or both.

"We are exposed here," Ishimaru said, looking around the quiet park.

"Think more of those ghouls are on the way?" I said as I decided fuck standing around and walked over to the nearest picnic table. If the vampire wanted to surprise attack me, he was welcome to try. I doubted I'd misread the situation that badly, however.

Tiger-Alek followed me, keeping his body between myself and the vampire. Which blocked my view of the vampire, but Ishimaru walked over to the other side of the table and hung back about three feet, choosing not to sit.

"Ghouls? I suppose that is not an incorrect name," he said. "There were four of them that I know of. Where is the fourth?"

Tiger-Alek snapped his jaws on air and gave his body a shake as he circled us.

"I think the fourth met a tiger," I said.

It certainly explained what had taken Alek so long to get over here. He must have gone after the one in the shop or caught it on its way out. I was relieved he wasn't hurt.

"Humans?" the vampire asked, glancing around again.

"All the bars are that way," I said, starting to gesture with my left arm. I regretted that immediately as pain lanced up my shoulder and made my head spin. "We're probably fine. I know the cops, anyway." Minor lie since I only knew the Sheriff, but even on a Saturday night, this part of town wouldn't see much traffic.

Tiger-Alek turned half away from us, facing toward the street but keeping the vampire in his peripheral vision.

"Nothing is getting by him, anyway," I said. Alek would hear any cars coming, and likely any undead too. I pictured all of us trying to duck behind trees or hiding under a picnic table and swallowed a giggle. I was definitely too tired for this shit.

"Tell me about the necromancer," I said.

"I cannot," Ishimaru said. He held up a hand to stop any response. "I have only vague memories of my time. It is all clouded with hunger and hatred."

"Whatever you remember, then?" I said. I wasn't sure why I was asking, though if I were honest with myself, I knew I was asking because I had a strong feeling this problem wasn't going to solve itself.

"He raises the dead. I remember books, many books, but he did not like me near him." Ishimaru bared his fangs again as he said that. "He was angry I could not make him one of us."

"He wants to be a vampire?" I said. "Is he human or like me? How old is he? What does he look like? Do you know his name?"

"Human and old for one of them. He is a white man. His blood is corrupted with magic now. But not like you. I imagine not many are like you."

I had no idea what to say to that, so I left it alone. "How long were you enslaved?"

"What is the year?"

I told him and he shook his head.

"Three years."

Not as long as I'd thought given the old-fashioned

appearance of his boots and trousers. Maybe the necromancer had liked to play dress-up. I buried that disturbing thought quickly.

"You said he was in his lair, but I was there. We never saw him. Or you."

"We were not there. The master," Ishimaru stopped and snarled. "The necromancer," he corrected himself. "He was away. I was sleeping, hidden away, for it was daylight."

I wondered what would have happened if we'd taken the left-hand path. More zombies, I guessed. Would we have found this lair?

"I messed up the place pretty good," I said aloud. "I doubt he'd stay there anymore."

"His special room is there, he will not leave it. Books, I remember all the books." Ishimaru shook his head again as though trying to clear it or shake loose a memory. Then he was still again and his dark gaze met mine. "He knows many things."

I got the impression he wasn't going to tell me more even if he were able. I supposed that if I'd been enslaved for a few years, I wouldn't be that thrilled to tell a random person all about it, either. The question was, what did I do about the necromancer? He was hours away from Wylde. I no longer had his jar of vampire heart, so it was possible he'd keep to himself.

Keep to himself and keep on raising zombies and making ghouls or whatever he was doing. I got why the Archivist was unhappy now. Also why he had needed me to do his dirty work. I could only imagine what would happen if someone enslaved Noah Grey. I also knew why Noah wanted me far away from the necromancer himself.

The necromancer wasn't a sorcerer, so he could be killed, though I imagined it wouldn't be easy since he sounded like a very powerful magic user with a lot of knowledge at his disposal. However, as a sorceress, I could eat his heart. Then all that knowledge would be mine, with sorcery behind it. My kind had no need of rituals if we had enough innate power, if we had knowledge and willpower to make things happen.

I had my magic comfort zone, my "A Box" as Alek called it. I liked fire or lightning or just throwing around magic force as its own thing. That was my go-to. My "B Box" had a lot more in it. I could fly or breathe under water or see in the dark. I'd cast huge-scale spells and slowed time. I'd even changed the course of time itself once, though I was never ever going to do that again.

There was no doubt in my mind that given the knowledge and desire, I could figure out necromancy. The real question was, why the fuck would I want to? Having my own personal zombie horde didn't sound exciting. Plus, if the feel and stench of the necromancer's magic was any indication, Ishimaru's descriptor of "corrupted with magic" was dead on target. I knew I wasn't that power-hungry. If I had been, I'd have just swallowed Samir's heart, the human world be damned.

Noah Grey, however, might believe that given the chance, I could choose to take the necromantic knowledge for myself. If a human necromancer could enslave a vampire, I shuddered to think what a sorcerer could do.

"You see it, then," Ishimaru said softly, breaking the rapid flow of my thoughts.

Tiger-Alek growled before I could form a response and I stood up from the bench as a car came up the hill. We all stood tensely watching as the car stopped in the church parking lot. Alek relaxed and turned to stare at the vampire the way a cat stares at a bug. The cat might not kill the bug, but it sure looks like it wants to.

Ishimaru ignored him.

"Jade?" Ezee said as he approached us. He had the katana in his hand, but looked more ready to draw it than hand it over as his nostrils flared.

I walked toward him, aware my back was to the vampire. I trusted that Alek would warn me if Ishimaru made a move. I held out my hand to Ezee.

"It's fine," I said. "We give him his sword, he leaves town. One less problem to worry about." I hoped.

Ezee raised an eyebrow. It was criminal that he looked so put together at two in the morning. I was in ripped and bloody sweats and a teeshirt with a belt hanging around my waist. He was wearing a pair of dark jeans, a racing jacket, and had not a hair out of place. I was glad he'd come without too much arguing.

Clearly exhaustion was making me maudlin. I took the sword and walked over to Ishimaru.

"Here," I said, offering it to him. "Our deal?"

"I will leave. You will go after the necromancer?" Ishimaru asked as he took the sword from my hand with both of his.

"Noah said he would handle it," I said, the best non-answer I could give.

Ishimaru nodded. "May I offer advice?"

"Can I stop you?" I muttered. I really wanted him

to go so I could get back to bed. Well, shower, then bed. I also still had to do something about the ripped up ghoul corpse and my shop's broken window. Damnit. I wasn't getting back to bed anytime soon.

Ishimaru unsheathed the blade and ran me through before I could blink or anyone could react. His breath was cool on my ear as he whispered, "Never trust a vampire, Jade Crow."

I used the wave of pain to pull my magic into a wall of force, thrusting the vampire away from me. Red spots danced in my vision as he flew backward. He caught himself on his feet, bloody sword still in hand. Shadows reached for him and in another beat of my racing heart, he was gone in the darkness as though he'd never been.

Alek caught me as I fell and Ezee's face swam into view above us.

"Just a flesh wound," I gasped out. Another ruined teeshirt, more blood lost. Awesomesauce.

"Shh, love," Alek said. "I have you."

"He was too fast," Ezee said, his voice full of the frustration I could see on Alek's unhappy face.

"He wasn't trying to kill me, just driving home a point," I said. Damn, chuckling at my own pun hurt.

"Seriously?" Ezee said.

I closed my eyes since looking up at them hurt too much and the world kept spinning. "I failed my will save," I muttered.

Alek lifted me up. "Taking you home," he said.

That sounded good to me. I could better direct clean up from there. Hopefully the bleeding would stop on the way. I gave in to the pain and exhaustion and let him carry me home. It was kind of our thing at this point. Like date night, but with a lot more bleeding and less consciousness.

It was close to six in the morning when I woke again and stumbled into the bathroom. My stomach and back were a mess of bruising. Alek had gotten my clothes off, I wasn't going to ask how, and cleaned me up. I had been semi-conscious for some of it, in and out because of the amount of pain I was in. I had no idea what vital bits the sword had cut through, but from how my guts felt, it hadn't missed much.

My left arm felt weak, but no longer a giant mass of agony, and my fingers responded to commands to open and close. My grip wasn't great yet.

Ezee had crashed in the guest room but my ablutions woke him and he came out into the living room as Alek set down a cup of tea and a plate of cold pizza in front of me.

"We tarped up the broken window," Ezee said before I could even ask. "Not much damage done inside, just some stuff knocked around. So don't panic."

"The ghoul in the park?"

"Buried it," Alek said. "Eat."

I obeyed, starving despite the pain in my belly. I needed to fortify myself for what I wanted to say next, since I knew Alek wasn't going to like it. I'd dozed on and off as I healed over the last few hours, but my mind had been at work even in my fitful dreams.

Washing down the last bite with the last swallow of tea, I looked from Ezee's calm, dark gaze to Alek's icy one. From his expression, I had a feeling that Alek knew me too damn well.

"I'm going after the necromancer," I said. "Today."

I'd decided it had to be today. If I gave him more time, he might move. I also didn't want Noah to try anything. I had a hunch those zombies wearing fatigues had once been in the employ of the Archivist, his first attempt to get the jar or whatever his true plan was. If he sent another group of armed men in to die and provide fresh bodies, it would only make my job tougher.

Alek picked up my empty plate and stalked back to the kitchen without a word. Yup. He knew me too well.

"Why?" Ezee asked. "You believe he'll come back?"

"I don't know," I said. "Perhaps. He knew where his jar was, or had a way to track it. He will find out he's failed if he didn't know already. But also, I can't ignore him now that I know he's out there, mere hours away. Where does he get his bodies for the zombies? What other monstrous critters is he constructing? What happens if he gets his hands on another vampire?" I shook my head. "Too many potential problems."

"So we go back and you what? Kill him?" Ezee asked.

"Yes," I said. "Though this all sounded less bloodthirsty in my head."

"He tried to kill you," Alek pointed out as he sank down on the couch beside me.

"After I invaded his home and took his stuff," I said. "Shit. Okay, so maybe we go try to talk to him?"

"I'll call Levi and Harper," Ezee said, pulling out his phone. He looked at me as though expecting me to object.

"Cool. I want another couple hours of sleep and then we should get going. I want to get there by midday. Full sunlight might impede his magic."

Ezee made the calls as I went and took another shower, hoping hot water would wash away my tiredness.

"Levi will be here in two hours. Harper says she'll sit this one out," Ezee said as I re-entered the living room.

"Oh," I said, trying to hide my disappointment. It was her decision, but it made me sad. She was always ragging on me about being the lone hero and not letting people help. I guessed things really had changed.

"Jade," Ezee said. "Relax, I'm joking. She said she'll be here in twenty."

I glared at him. "I'm tired, don't do that to me."

"Go get more rest, crankypants," Ezee said.

I took the professor's advice.

"You're letting us come with you? No arguing about how dangerous it is?" Harper said, squinting at me.

Everyone was assembled and dressed for battle, such

as it were. I'd pulled on the toughest jeans I owned and a plain shirt I didn't mind getting burned up or ripped to pieces, though I hoped none of that would happen again. Harper was wearing a pair of BDU's that she might have borrowed from Ezee from the looks of it, since he had a similar pair on now. She, Levi, and Ezee had leather jackets, though the styles varied, and all had machetes looped through their belts with cord. They'd even brought an extra weapon for Alek.

"Where do you get that many machetes on a Sunday morning?" I asked.

I'd gone back to sleep and slept longer than I meant to. We were getting a late start, but would still reach the house in daylight at least.

"I know a guy," Levi said with a grin.

"Ha," I said. "Okay, the plan is we go down the ladder we came out and head back to that intersection where we went right instead of left."

"You going to use the jar to track?" Ezee asked, pointing at the kitchen table.

I had dismantled the jar as best I could to get the spinny bit on top off. I didn't need the whole jar to cast a tracking spell, just the dial thing would work well enough. I hoped. If the necromancer wasn't the one who had made the jar, it might be useless.

"Just this part," I said, pulling the dial out of my pocket. "But the range on spells like this isn't great. It'll be easier to see if it can lead us once we're there. I don't even know yet if it'll point at the necromancer."

Alek's phone rang and he mouthed "Rachel" at me and ducked into our bedroom to take the call. I followed him after a minute.

"Thank you," he said to the phone and hung up.

"She okay?" I went to him and wrapped my arms around his waist. His neck was mostly healed now, only a pink scar remaining.

"Calling to ask if we knew about the vandalism at the park," he said. He tucked his phone into his pocket and returned my hug. "I forgot to mention it when I warned her about the store window."

"Lara's explaining the shop damage as a remodeling issue we just now caught. She wanted to open today, so I'm going to let her." Thank the universe for good employees.

"Are you healed enough to do this?" Alek said. His lips were a tight line in his face, his eyes full of unhappiness.

I rolled my eyes at him and then head-butted his

chest, ignoring the twinge of pain that sent down my left arm.

"I can't just leave this mess for someone else to clean up," I said. "You know that."

"You lovebirds going to move it, or are we heading out alone?" Levi said, leaning into the bedroom.

"Let me grab a change of clothes to stick in the car, and then I'm ready," I said, breaking away from Alek.

Levi had brought a bigger car, which we all appreciated, Alek most of all since even in the front seat it was still a crunch for his six-foot-six frame. Weapons went into the trunk along with a thick coil of rope, a couple tarps and a change of clothing for me.

"I brought real lock picks," Harper said. "So should it go faster if we have to open more doors."

"We got a tank, a rogue, a mage, and two fighters. We'll be fine," Levi said.

I snorted as I climbed into the back seat. "You two are fighters? More like torch-bearers."

"Levi did bring a flashlight," Ezee said.

"No badmouthing the driver," Levi said as he turned the key in the ignition.

It was a long drive.

The house looked much like we'd left it, the backside caving and sagging. There was no more smoke hovering over the ground to show us where the trap door was beyond the house, but it wasn't tough to find. We just followed our own tracks back across the dusty ground.

The sun was sinking slowly toward the western horizon but still warm on our backs as we pulled open the trap door. The heat wasn't helping the rotting flesh chunks that still decorated the area from my phoenix impression the day before. The scent of rot and death was as pervasive as the dust. The shifters bent and listened at the ladder.

"I hear nothing," Alek said. The other three nodded.

"Looks good to me, guys," Harper said, winking at me in an exaggerated fashion.

"Tank goes first?" Levi bowed to Alek and swept his arm out in invitation.

"I go first," I said as I stepped up to the hole. "I'm the immortal one, remember?"

"You can still get hurt," Alek said.

"So can you," I countered. I didn't wait for them to keep arguing with me but stepped down onto the ladder.

Rung by rung I descended down the ladder. I hung at the bottom, my feet on the last rung and looked around. The walls were blackened by the fire and corpses decorated the floor. I'd smoked at least a dozen zombies from the look of it. They were mostly burned up, zombies apparently being highly flammable, but here and there I could make out bones among the charred remains.

"Lot of bodies, nothing moving," I said, knowing my friends would hear me. "Dropping down."

I let go of the ladder and jumped down to the floor. My feet almost skidded out from under me on a leg bone but I waved my arms around in a very heroic manner and caught my balance.

No movement as the soot settled. These zombies were truly dead. The electric sconces in here were still lit, giving the room an incongruously cozy glow. I moved away from the ladder and toward the hallway we'd come down. Behind me I heard Alek drop down with a muttered Russian curse, then the sounds of the others following suit.

I pulled the dial out of my pocket and summoned my magic. I focused on the metal in my hand, willing it to seek out the one who had used it the most, guessing that would be the necromancer. The pull was immediate and strong. My guess wasn't wrong.

"This way," I said. I moved the dial to my left hand and drew the Alpha and Omega.

With a glance over my shoulder to reassure myself my friends were following, I started back down the hallway and into the dungeon.

The dial pulled us along the hallways until we reached the junction again and turned into the unfamiliar hall. Nothing rose up to try and stop us and the place was eerily silent except for the sound of our shoes on the stone floor.

The hall here was reinforced with wooden scaffolding and larger than the ones we had been in before. The floor sloped downward and we descended. My hand started to ache from holding the dial thingy, my partially healed muscles lodging a protest against being forced to do work for this long. The hallway went deep and it felt like we were walking miles underground, but I knew some of that was because of the unchanging perspective of the hallway itself.

"Wait," Alek murmured behind me.

I halted and stood, trying to breathe quietly so I could listen. The lights were on here as well, but spaced far apart. We stood in a section of near darkness in the gap between two of the sconces. I felt almost like I was on a mission in Skyrim, only I didn't have a bow.

"Behind us," Alek said.

"What? For those without super hearing," I muttered, my eyes straining to see anything ahead of us. Turning around wouldn't help, I'd just see Alek's body. He took up a lot of space even in human form.

"Sounds like zombies," Ezee said.

"Keep moving," Levi said. "They aren't close yet."

I started forward again. Three sconces from where we'd stopped, a door appeared. This one was newer than the others, its metal not rusted and the wood untouched by rot or water damage. It had a keyhole but no handle.

"Harper," I said. "Rogue up."

The hallway was wide enough she could get past everyone easily. She pulled a small leather pouch from one of her cargo pockets and unrolled a set of lockpicks.

"If we don't get eaten by zombies," I whispered to her, "you have to teach me how to do that."

She chuckled and got to work. With the proper tools she had the door open within a couple minutes.

"Helps to hear really well," she said as she stood up.

The door eased silently open away from us. Nothing leapt out to attack us so I moved inside. The vestibule opened up quickly into a large rectangular chamber that was lit by a huge chandelier high above. Discarded coffins lined the sides of the chamber in varying states of decay. The smell of rotting wood, putrid flesh, and mildew was strong enough that all of us were gagging. Swirling around it all was the stench of the necromancer's magic, though I saw no bodies. But with so much clutter along the sides of the chamber and shitty overhead lighting, an army could have hidden in here.

"That's not promising," Levi said as we fanned out into the room.

"This guy has seriously weird decorating tastes," Ezee said.

There was another door in the far end and my tracking spell was still pulling my arm that direction. I adjusted my grip on the Alpha and Omega and pointed.

"Spell says that way," I said.

"Should I lock the door behind us?" Harper suggested.

"That traps us," Alek said with a head shake. He rolled his shoulders, muscles and sinew crackling in the dead silence of the room. Good to know I wasn't the only who was tense.

"Wedge with a piece of coffin?" Levi said.

Ezee and Levi pulled over a chunk of wood that had once been a simple pine box. Some of the coffins were nice, modern contraptions with silk linings. Many were not as nice, just simple wooden boxes, quite a few half-rotted away or smashed.

The door kind of secured, we grouped up and picked our way across the hall.

I felt the slight hum of magic right before I stepped onto the ward. I tried to hop backward but Alek was too close and I bumped into him. My foot came down and a deep chime like an old brass bell reverberated around the chamber.

"Forgot to check for traps," Harper said. I glanced back and saw wild grins on the faces of my friends. Alek's expression was more resigned but there was a light in his eyes.

Coffins started to move, lids sliding off the whole ones. Broken wood was shoved aside as the dead hiding beneath the mess came to life again.

My estimation that an army could have hidden in here wasn't inaccurate.

Not waiting, I charged the nearest zombie and dusted it with my sword. Alek came to my side and smashed in another zombie's head as it clawed at me.

"To the door," I yelled as I started swinging. It was difficult to fight zombies and keep the tracking spell going, so I gave up and dropped the spell, jamming the dial into my pocket to free my left hand. Through that door was where I needed to go. I'd worry about the details post-zombie fight.

We reached the door. Behind me I heard Ezee cry out in pain. A zombie had gotten around Levi's machete swing and sunk its claws into Ezee's side. He kicked it away and smashed in its skull as it fell back.

"I'm okay," he said. Blood darkened his leather jacket.

Two more zombies leapt down from a stack of coffins. There was too much stuff in here to use fire to deflect them. We had to rely on our melee skills. Levi slashed right through the arm of a zombie but it kept coming, slamming into him and knocking him back. Another tried to bite into his leg, but Ezee was there, stomping down with his boot and crushing its skull with shifter strength.

"Harper, get that open." I shoved away from the door. My sword was the most effective thing against the undead since I didn't need a headshot to kill them.

"Back up," Alek told Ezee and Levi as they scrambled to reach us.

We formed a half circle around Harper as she took up a litany of curses by the door.

The zombies kept coming, charging one after the other into my sword swing. I had to be very careful how I used the blade, fighting in close quarters with Alek to one side. If I nicked him, he'd die. I felt more than saw Alek move away from me as Ezee cried out in pain again.

Dusting the zombie in front of me, I turned my head. Ezee was down, more blood on his right leg as well as his ripped jacket. Levi and Alek had closed the gap he left, putting him back behind them.

Five more zombies crawled out into the open. Rotting flesh hung from their bones. These sad creatures were very decayed, older than the corpses littering the ground in front of us. They moved jerkily, bones scraping the debris as they tried to charge us.

I ran forward, ignoring Alek's yell. I could take five skeletons and I wanted nobody else to get hurt. The first reached me and I severed its arm with an uppercut, using both hands on the blade. I reversed the swing and cut back across the zombie's body.

This time I was ready for it when it turned to dust and able to stop the momentum. One of the skeletons had gone past me but two more tried to close. I swung the Alpha and Omega in a wide arc parallel to the ground, slashing through their rotting torsos. Chips of bone flaked away in the path of the blade and gore spattered me as I flicked the blade back for a reverse swing.

The zombies dusted before I could connect again, their gaping mouths giving them an almost comical expression of permanent surprise as they turned to grit.

The last zombie lurched at me from the side, its claw-like hands swiping at me. I danced backward, tripping over a piece of wood. The zombie crashed down onto me. Its teeth sank into my forearm as I tried to bring the sword around and stab it. The blade scraped along the exposed bone of its loose arm. Then it was dust coating my body instead of rotting flesh and bone.

I scrambled to my feet.

"Got the door," Harper called out.

No more movement in the hall that I could see. Hopefully we'd killed all the zombies.

Ezee had shifted to his coyote form, which meant he was more hurt than he had let on. Levi had a gash in his left leg but was still in human form. He leaned heavily on his machete like it was a cane, however.

"You okay?" I asked as I stumbled back to them.

"That was stupid," Alek said. He looked unharmed, to my relief.

"I've got a magic sword," I said in my defense.

"You're bleeding."

I twisted my arm around to get a look at the bite. It was ugly, but nothing too serious. My poor left arm was taking a beating.

"I won't be in about two minutes," I said. "Let's get out of here."

Alek snarled, his gaze moving past me, back the way we had come.

The door we had blocked slammed open. Three of the ghoulish demonic creatures like the ones we had fought in the park the night before charged into the room. They hissed when they saw us. Then two more came in behind them.

Five. Ghouls. Shit.

"Door, go, now," I said.

"What are those?" Levi asked as we backed into the hallway beyond.

I went in last, watching the ghouls as they picked their way across toward us, seemingly in no hurry. That worried me even more.

"Demonic ghoul things?" I said. "Those are what attacked last night. They are kind of smart, so look out."

"And fast," Alek added.

The hallway we backed into was about ten feet wide and again reinforced with scaffolding like you'd see in a mine shaft. The ceiling was high enough here that Alek didn't have to stoop to get under the beams.

It was too wide to make a good stand. The ghouls would be able to get to us in pairs and we'd be hampered by the enclosed space.

"So they die?" Harper asked.

The ghoul in front stopped and hissed at me from just a dozen feet off now. Its eyes glowed brighter.

"Do enough damage, yeah," I said. Or hit them with the Alpha and Omega, which was shining with blue light again.

I let my magic pour into my blood. This room would go up in spectacular fashion if I used enough fire. The question was, would the ghouls make it to me before I could burn them. If I stayed in the doorway, the space was narrow enough they couldn't get past me.

"If you burn room, we might not be able to get out," Alek said softly behind me.

I felt his warmth at my back as his hand gently touched my shoulder. He had a point, alas. We stared down the ghouls as the magic sang in my blood. They seemed content to wait out of sword range for us to act. Too bad they were smart enough not to charge the armed woman standing in a narrow doorway.

"I will shift and fight them," Alek said. "Move, Jade."

"Nope, vetoed. I know you are a badass but nope."

"I killed two last night," he said. I heard the frustrated growl in his voice.

"There's five," I said. "They could surround you out there. Nope." I couldn't shake a vision of Alek being clawed to pieces by misshapen creatures with glowing red eyes.

"We can hold the door," Harper said.

"No you can't." I shook my head. "They are ridiculously strong."

"So are we," Levi said.

"And after?"

"You go find the necromancer, we'll hold the door." Levi's voice was tight with pain.

"That phrase is never going to be the same again, is it?" Harper said.

"If I back out of this doorway, they might charge before we get it shut," I said. This door had opened into the hallway, not the room.

"Distract them?" Harper suggested.

It was worth a shot. Better than standing here until we all died of boredom or did something stupid. I wasn't going to let them hold the door while I ran off to find the wizard, but maybe once we had it shut we could get it locked again.

"Ok, wait for my signal. Back up, get ready," I said.

I sent my magic out from me in dual tendrils. It was tough to do it without using gestures, but my left arm was aching badly against my side and my right held the

ANNIE BELLET

sword in what I hoped was a seriously threatening manner. I had to do this without a somatic component. I was a big girl sorceress, I could manage.

I wrapped my magic tentacles around two intact, heavy-looking coffins to either side of the wedge of ghouls.

"Now," I yelled as I mentally yanked on the coffins, visualizing them slamming together right on the front ghoul's stupid toothy face.

The coffins scraped along the ground, moving far more slowly than I had envisioned. They slammed together as I backed up quickly, but not on the ghoul. The ghouls sprang across the remaining dozen feet just as the door banged shut in their faces, almost catching me as I flattened myself to the wall to let it pass.

Levi and Alek threw their bodies against the door and it held as a ghoul smashed into it from the other side. The whole hallway shook with the impact and dust trickled down from the rocky ceiling.

"Not going to hold forever," Levi gasped out.

"Relock it," I told Harper.

"That won't do much, it's just a bolt in there. Might rip out of the frame if they keep that up."

"It'll buy us time to run," I said.

"We'll buy you time. Go," Harper said. She ducked under Alek's arm and put her weight into the shaking door.

Coyote-Ezee shoved his shoulder into the door alongside Harper. The wood was thick and banded with iron. With three shifters leaning all their weight into it, it was holding. For now.

"Come," Alek said.

"I'm not splitting the party," I said.

"Jade, trust us. We're not helpless," Harper said through gritted teeth.

I reached a compromise in my head as I turned and looked down the hall. There was a bend just ahead and the light was brighter in that direction.

"It's dangerous, take this," I said, managing a smile as I held out the Alpha and Omega to my best friend. "Pointy end goes in the other guy."

"Thanks," Harper said. Her green eyes glinted in the light of the blade as she gripped it. The sword kept glowing and stayed in sword form, so I hoped that meant it accepted her. With it, they stood a chance.

"Seriously, don't cut anything you don't intend to be dead," I said.

"Go," Levi said as another body slammed the door from the other side.

I started down the hallway. Alek followed.

"They might need you," I said to him as he fell into step beside me.

"You might need me," Alek answered.

I started to reach into my pocket for the dial so I could re-cast the spell as we went around the bend. Then I stopped. The hall opened into a room dead ahead. We walked forward cautiously and looked into the huge circular chamber.

We had found the necromancer. And... a sheep?

15

The chamber looked like something out of Beauty and the Beast. Shelves full of books lined the circular walls, with ladders at intervals providing access to the higher ones. There was a platform carved into the far wall that had a bed on it. I couldn't see all the way back to know if there was an exit up there or more rooms. The floor of the chamber was tiled with green stone in an intricate pattern. In the center was a circle inlaid with copper with more copper lines in a wheel spoke pattern out from the center. Staked in the center was a sheep, a loop of rope around its neck tied to a ring embedded in the floor.

The necromancer stood behind a giant desk at the

back of the chamber, a revolver in one shaking hand. He was an old man, as the vampire had said, with papery white skin, pale terrified eyes, and a comb-over of salt and pepper hair plastered to his sweaty head.

I held up my hands, but mentally readied a shield in case he tried to shoot at us.

"Hey," I called out. "Let's talk."

The necromancer nodded vigorously, though he didn't lower the gun.

The room was hazy with incense smoke and as I walked carefully into the chamber, I noticed enclosed incense burners hanging from chains off metal hooks at intervals around the room. It reminded me of the homes I'd been in where the human was a life-long smoker. Always trying to hide the smell with other smells.

I skirted the copper circle. The sheep started bleating or baaing or whatever you call the horrible noise sheep make. Beside me, Alek growled. The sheep shut up instantly. I glanced at my mate to confirm he was still in human form.

"What do you want?" the necromancer said as we stopped about ten feet from him.

"Call off the ghouls," I said.

"The what?" He looked genuinely confused for a moment and then comprehension dawned on his face. "I can't. They are programmed by the spell that made them to kill anything that comes down here that isn't me."

"The sheep is alive," I said. Why did he have a sheep? I figured we'd get to that.

The necromancer gave me a look like he was wondering how I'd made it to adulthood. "There is another way out," he said, pointing at the ladder that led up to his loft. "If you promise to leave in peace, you can use it."

"Can't do that," I said. "You attacked me, sent those things after me."

"You stole my vampire," he said.

"You were enslaving him," I countered.

"It's a vampire, who cares?" The gun dipped. His arm was getting tired. Didn't surprise me, it takes a lot of energy and strength to hold a gun steady for a long period.

"The vampire who hired me to get the jar, clearly," I said. Technically Noah hadn't hired me, but I doubted technicalities were important right then.

The necromancer's tongue flicked out over his thin

lips. His teeth and tongue were greenish-black. I was guessing this guy didn't have much of a social life. Maybe that was what the sheep was for. I shoved away that thought as soon as it surfaced. Ick.

"It is not enough you've ruined my house and killed my experiments?" he asked. "I am dying. The young don't understand what it is like to have your body fail. Leave me to die in peace."

I glanced at Alek, but he was no help. He stared at the necromancer with a look of mild disgust on his face. I'd come down here with the intention of killing this guy, but I hadn't expected to kind of feel sorry for him.

"What about all those zombies? They were people once, too," I said.

"They died on their own, didn't you see the coffins? I don't kill people, I work with the dead." His greenish tongue flicked over his lips again and his eyes darted to the side, glancing at the sheep.

"Lies," Alek said.

"I only kill to defend myself," the necromancer said, his nervous pale gaze settling on Alek. "Those armed men that came before you. That's all."

"Lie," Alek said.

That made me feel a little less pity for the old man. He had to die. If I left him here, there was no way to know how many people he'd kill before the Archivist sent enough men to stop him, or old age and illness finally took him down. The necromancer knew where I lived, as well. He could be the type to hold a grudge.

Killing someone like this in cold blood wasn't my jam. I glanced at Alek again. It was his, I knew. He'd executed people for the Council many times. Could I order him to kill? I knew he would do it. Hell, he was probably just waiting for me to say "go" before he struck.

The necromancer acted while I hung on the edge of indecision. He swung the gun up and pulled the trigger.

I slammed my magical shield into place as soon as I saw his arm moving, but the necromancer hadn't shot at us. He unloaded five shots into the sheep.

Before the sixth shot went off, Alek went around my shield, leapt over the desk and on top of him. He smashed the necromancer's arm against the shelves and the gun went flying. Alek hauled the necromancer out from behind the desk and shook him like a rat.

"Please please please," the little old man whined.

I looked to where the sheep lay in a spreading pool of blood.

"What did you do that for?" I asked.

The stench of necromantic power washed over us in a nauseating wave. The sheep's blood ran into the copper channels of the circle and the ground started to shake. Behind me, Alek cried out and I saw the necromancer go flying as Alek tossed him away.

A small knife stuck in Alek's arm where the necromancer had stabbed him. Old age and treachery, I thought. Get you every time. Alek ripped the knife out with a snarl.

The floor kept shaking and I had trouble maintaining my balance. The incense gathered like a cloud inside, swirling around and obscuring the center. Summoning my magic, I sent a wave of power at the circle but it was rebuffed by the lines of copper. The force knocked me onto my ass.

Alek shifted to tiger, leaping past me as the smoke swirled outward and abruptly dissipated. A huge creature remained. It was nearly twice the size of tiger-Alek, with the same shiny grey skin as the ghouls. It had six legs that all terminated in big clawed hands, and a long barbed tail. Its head was something from an

H.R. Giger nightmare, with venomous-looking teeth and four sets of glowing red eyes embedded deep in its shiny carapace-like forehead.

And me, in a room full of paper. If I wasn't careful, I was going to get us all killed. No fire, check.

The monster went for tiger-Alek. Alek dodged its swiping claws and raked its shoulder. Black ichor spurted but its tail came around and slammed into Alek's body, throwing him to the side. He twisted, cat-quick, and landed with a snarl as the monster snapped on empty air where he had been.

I gathered magic into my hands, pouring every ounce of power I could muster into a giant ball of whirling death. The monster was ignoring me for the moment, to its detriment. I prepared to throw the energy ball, yelling as I did so to get the monster's attention.

"Kamehameha!"

The necromancer hit me in the side with an incense burner just as I released the ball. The blow knocked me sideways as my ribs cracked and the air whooshed out of my lungs in a painful gasp. The ball flew high, smashing into the shelves beyond. It started to rain paper.

I rolled to the side, struggling to catch my breath. The necromancer came at me again with the burner, swinging it like a mace at my head. I kicked hard, connecting with his left knee as he closed the distance. His knee went the wrong direction and I heard a sickening snap. With a scream, he collapsed.

I crab walked back, away from the necromancer, leaving him to writhe in pain. My back hit the desk. Tiger-Alek was still fighting the monster, darting in and twisting away, blood dotting his white fur. He was moving well, so I hoped the injuries weren't too awful.

I needed my sword but leaving Alek to battle alone while I ran back down the hall sounded like a terrible plan. I'd left it with Harper for a reason. If I went and took it, Alek could lose the fight while I ran. If I took it, Harper and the twins could lose the fight at the door with no simple and quick way to kill the ghouls.

"Damn sword is a crutch" I muttered to myself. I couldn't rely on having a magic weapon that killed everything for me. I'd gotten by without it before.

My ribs felt like someone had used me like a soccer ball, but I struggled to my feet, breathing as shallowly as possible.

Alek had the monster spinning this way and that,

using claw and tail to try to pin the giant tiger down. He had it utterly distracted for the moment, and mostly held in the same spot.

We'd fought huge things before. I couldn't just burn it down, so I had to think outside the box. We were in a box of sorts in this room. A box with a stone floor.

Kneeling back down, I glanced at the necromancer. He was lying on his side, gasping. He watched the fight with a crazy look on his face.

I pooled my magic in my hands again, the power flowing through my blood pushing back the pain and exhaustion I felt. I'd used a lot of magic over the last few days and my body was feeling every phantom injury I'd had to heal that weekend. Red dots littered my vision. I blinked them away.

I'd only done this once, on a stone monster out in the River of No Return wilderness, but I remembered how it had felt and used that memory to enforce my will. My magic plunged into the stone floor and rippled in a wave toward the monster. The floor felt like solid bedrock beneath the stone tiles covering it. I visualized my magic spreading into a circle around the monster, still deep beneath the floor. I sealed the circle and spread my magic out to fill it.

With a deep breath my ribs instantly regretted I'd taken, I used my magic to turn the stone to sand and yanked downward as I did. The tiles beneath the monster collapsed as they dissolved into sand. It tried to leap away as its back legs were trapped in the quicksand but I pulled harder, pushing my magic deeper into the bedrock.

The monster sank up to its last set of clawed legs with a hideous screech. I was losing control of the spell, my magic felt like burning ropes of acid in my hands. As soon as the shoulders of the monster hit the sand and fell under, I pictured stone again, hard perfect, gleaming stone. The sand solidified around the monster, crushing it.

Tiger-Alek leapt as soon as he saw the ground change from sand to rock. With paws bigger than my head and claws longer than my fingers, he ripped into the exposed head of the monster, tearing into its dying face with fury. Ichor and chunks of grey flesh flew. Alek really hated undead, from what I could tell.

I staggered to my feet, my vision now full of dancing red dots. I was going to pay for all this magic use, and soon.

But not yet.

A yell rang down the hallway.

"Go," I called out to Alek, pointing toward the hall.

He abandoned the dead monster and snarled at me. Red blood and black ichor decorated his white fur. There was a long shallow gash on his left side.

"Go," I said again. "Please." This was not the time for arguing. I could handle an old man with a busted knee, though I wouldn't underestimate him again.

With another snarl, Alek sprang away and disappeared down the hall.

I turned to the necromancer. He was edging away from me with wide eyes.

"I almost pitied you," I told him. I kicked the incense burner out of the way. It had fallen open and papers smoldered where the burning coal had fallen.

"Put out the fire," he gasped, pointing to the coal.

I stomped down on it, grinding my foot in. Then I walked forward again, advancing on him as he wiggled across the tiles along the shelves.

"What are you?" he asked. "You did that?" His pale eyes flicked to the embedded monster in the now smooth, solid stone floor.

"I'm a sorceress," I said. "I thought you knew that."

"I thought that was a myth," he said. His greenish-black tongue darted out over his lips again.

"Nope," I said, stopping just short of his feet. He had nowhere to go now, his back against the shelves.

"You could help me," he said, his eyes still lit with inner madness. "Help me raise her."

"Say what?" I said. "Raise who?"

"Lilith," he said as though that explained it.

One of Tess's memories swam up in my head. "Mother of demons, Lilith?" I guessed.

"Mother of vampires," the necromancer said. "She's the only one who can make a new vampire. If we raise her, we can live forever!"

It seemed cruel to tell an old, injured man, necromancer or no, that one of us was already going to live forever. Though with my lifestyle, I wasn't entirely sure that would truly happen.

"As a vampire? No thanks," I said.

He spat to one side. "The young always think they'll live forever anyway," he said with disgust.

"I'm almost fifty," I pointed out. "Not that young." By human standards. I left that part out.

He looked up at me, skepticism writ large on his pale face. He really didn't know much about sorcerers. His watery grey eyes flicked toward the shelf beside him. I followed his glance but saw only a double stack of books.

"I could teach you so much," he tried again. His hand inched toward the shelf.

"Whatever is there won't help you," I said. I was going to have to kill him. I saw that now, but that didn't make it easier.

First I had decide if I was going to eat his heart. I didn't want to. But he knew things about vampires that I might find useful if I'd gone and made enemies with one, or potentially two of them. On the other hand, I didn't want to be a necromancer. This kind of magic didn't just smell awful, it felt wrong. Corrupted. Ishimaru had used the right word.

"You've read all these books?" I asked, stalling for more time.

Another shout rang down the hall and I turned my head for just a second.

The necromancer pulled the gun out from between the stacks of books as I turned my head back.

I dove at him, magic coming to my hands as I jammed my palm over the muzzle of the small revolver. I wrapped power around the gun even as he pulled the trigger. The bullet locked into the cylinder and the gun recoiled out of his hand as it failed to fire.

Forming violet claws around my right hand, I plunged them into the old man's chest. He screamed, greenish spittle misting my face as I crushed bone to get to his heart. I ripped it out and he collapsed onto the floor beneath me. Kneeling over him, I held his heart, my magic swirling around it, keeping it beating.

His heart was the same greenish-black as his tongue had been.

All the knowledge in this room was here, in my hand. A lifetime of studying. Knowledge of vampires and who knew what else.

The temptation to just crush the heart and leave was strong. I could read these books, gain the knowledge that way, but I knew even as I thought it that there was zero chance that Noah would let this place stand once the necromancer was gone. He'd take the books or destroy them. He was the Archivist, after all.

I knew my decision. I'd known it all along, but had to spend the moments trying to talk myself out of it. The knowledge and power in this heart might save my life and the lives of people I loved someday.

I bit into it. It tasted worse than it looked. I made myself swallow the heart along with the bile that rose as soon as the bitter, rotting flesh hit my tongue. The stomach acid marginally improved the flavor, that's how awful it was.

The necromancer was dead. I rose to my feet and dropped the remains of his heart onto his body. Greasy magic burst in my chest as the transfer of power took hold of me, but I stayed upright through sheer will. I called to Wolf in my mind and she was there, herding the new power into the silver circle in my head where I'd corralled all the memories from the people I'd killed and hearts I had taken. Tess. Haruki. Barnes. Now... Robert Loughlin. The necromancer had a name, of course. He'd had a life. I'd look at it later. Much, much later.

I touched my talisman, feeling the warm, hard bump of Samir's heart stone there, still embedded in the one spot on the die.

With the necromancer's knowledge and power safely shut away, I looked around the room. So many books. I reached for my magic again. It was sluggish in responding, my body bone-weary even with the influx of fresh power from the necromancer.

"Jade?" Alek appeared in the hall entrance.

I walked across the room toward him. "Everyone okay?"

"The ghouls stopped moving. Harper killed one. Levi was bitten but he shifted. He will be fine," Alek said quickly, seeing my expression. "It is over?"

"It is over," I said. I was glad he hadn't seen what I had done, though I knew I would tell him. Knowing Alek, he guessed.

He confirmed as much as he reached out and brushed his thumb against my lips, wiping away greenish blood.

I used my already dirty teeshirt as a napkin and wiped my face.

"Better?" I asked.

"Your breath is awful," Alek said with a slight smile.

Harper appeared behind him with an over-sized coyote and wolverine in tow.

"Here," she said. She reached into her pocket and pulled out a piece of gum.

"Gum?" I took it, unwrapping it and popping it into my mouth. Cinnamon. It would have to do.

"Gamer's motto," she said with a grin. "Be prepared."

"That's the Boy Scout motto," I said, chewing. The gum was helping get rid of the rotting flesh and trash taste.

"We should go," Alek said.

I nodded. "I'll meet you at the ladder. I have to clean up down here." I motioned to the books. "Can't leave this for anyone to find."

"Here," Harper said, holding out the Alpha and Omega. It was back in dagger form.

I took it and slid it into its sheath, relieved to have it back.

"Yell when you get through the coffin room," I told them.

Alek called out a minute or so later and I pulled on my magic. Fire sang in my blood as I channeled beams of flame up into the bookshelves. I felt like I was committing a worse crime than murder, but it had to be done.

When the smoke grew too thick for me to see, I backed out of the room and jogged down the hall. Smoke followed me, hungry for an outlet.

I torched the coffin room as well after picking my way over the inert bodies of the dead zombies and ghouls. Better safe than sorry. That done, I summoned what I could of my remaining energy and tried to ignore the deep ache in my ribs as I jogged down the halls to rejoin my companions.

The dungeon was cleared. I wished I could feel

triumph or accomplishment, but I felt only exhaustion and a hollow grief of a sort I had no name for. I knew only that there would be a price for my actions. There always was.

"Not today," I told myself. We were safe. For now.

16

Ezee and Levi both had to shift to get up the ladder. Levi's right arm was a mess of crushed bone that oozed fresh blood. Ezee wasn't as bad off, a couple deep gouges in his leg and side. At least he didn't start bleeding again as he let Alek lift him up to the ladder's bottom rungs.

"Levi, you okay?" I said, wincing at the sight of his wounds. Junebug was going to kill me.

"Flesh wound," he said with a forced grin. His piercings glinted in the dim light. "I can climb with one arm, I think."

He proved it by scrambling up the ladder after jumping and catching it with his left arm.

"Show off," Harper muttered, rolling her eyes. She went up next.

Alek lifted me up and climbed behind me. I was running on fumes by then, but told myself that if Levi could climb with one arm, I could manage with two, no matter how leaden my muscles felt.

It was dark as I emerged. Levi and Ezee had shifted back to their animal forms. Levi's wolverine had a distinct limp, but at least this way he wasn't bleeding anymore. Harper had the flashlight on her and clicked it on, leading the way back to where we'd left the car.

"I'll drive," she offered as we rounded the house. "Levi already gave me the keys."

I just nodded, though she couldn't see it.

We walked down the driveway and Harper jerked to a halt right in front of me. Ezee and Levi fanned out to the sides, teeth bared. I looked up from where I'd been putting one foot in front of the other.

A dark SUV was parked behind our vehicle. A tall man in a suit stood by the passenger door on the driver's side. He was holding an electric lamp as though he'd been born to be a lamppost.

Noah Grey climbed out of the vehicle and waited in that pool of light for us to approach.

"Get behind me," I told my friends.

"I told you to leave this alone," the Archivist said as I walked forward to meet him.

"You know me better than that," I said, hoping he didn't know me too well.

"You had the jar," he said. "You lied to me."

"You lied to me first," I said. It had sounded less petulant-child-like in my head. "I didn't know what was in that jar. You would have done the same thing. I thought the heart might be some poor sorcerer stuck in there. Until I knew, I couldn't hand it over. The vampire is free now, by the way, so you don't have to worry about that."

"He is free?" Noah looked thoughtful, his air of anger fading. "You should not have lied to me."

"You should have told me what I was up against before it tried to kill me. You should also have told me that you'd sent in armed men and failed, badly. Thanks for that, by the way. I really enjoyed all those extra zombies we had to fight."

"Where is the warlock?" Noah said. His eyes glinted like a beetle's carapace in the soft lamp light.

"Necromancer," I said. He flinched slightly at the word, the second time I'd ever seen an involuntary motion from a vampire. I was going to have to start a bingo card. "You mean that, and I quote, one you 'took care of?'"

"Jade Crow," he said, his voice an impatient hiss. Noah didn't seem to appreciate my excellent memory. Or maybe it was just that I was throwing his own lies in his face.

"He's dead," I said.

"How did he die?"

I'd known that question was coming. My exhaustion was a boon here as my heart was too weary to get excited and start leaping around. I had no adrenaline left.

"He tried to shoot me," I said, sticking close to the truth. "I crushed him with magic." Technically not a lie. One very slender technicality.

Noah peered at me, his lips flattening into a tight line before peeling back and revealing his fangs.

"Crushed him?" he repeated.

"I'm not stupid, Noah," I said. I channeled my tired frustration into my tone. "There's no more necromancer. I burned his books, so that knowledge is gone to ash where it belongs. Go and check yourself, I don't care. But first move your damn car, because we're hurt, we're tired, and we're going the fuck home."

He stared at me a moment longer and then nodded slowly. He gestured to the lamp post guy to move aside and then he got back in. The SUV moved back, pulling to the side of the driveway and leaving us enough room to turn around and leave.

Harper unlocked Levi's car and Alek opened the doors but we quickly realized the twins weren't going to fit if they were both shifted. Shifter coyotes are the size of a German Shepherd, and shifter wolverines are closer to a Saint Bernard. Ezee shifted.

"I'm less hurt," he said as Levi stared up at him with a huff.

Levi didn't argue, probably because he couldn't speak in this form, and jumped into the vehicle.

Alek went around to the passenger seat but stood alert instead of getting in.

I looked back at the vampire's vehicle. Noah had unrolled the window and leaned slightly out. I walked a couple steps closer and folded my arms across my aching chest.

"We will check the house and grounds," the Archivist said. "If it is not as you say..." he trailed off, the threat implied.

"Knock yourself out," I said. I turned my back on

him, ignoring the itch of danger between my shoulder blades.

"Good night, Jade Crow," the Archivist called after me. "I will see you again."

I spun back. I was sick of vampires and games.

"How about not?" I said. "I'm declaring Wylde a vampire-free zone starting now. If I need you, I know where you live." I didn't mean that last to sound quite as ominous as it came out, but I left it hanging in the air between us as I turned again and stalked to the car.

I slammed the door shut and did not look at the Archivist again as Harper turned the car on, pulled a three-point turn, and sped away into the darkness.

"Call to warn me if Junebug loses her peacenik ways and goes on the war path when she sees you," I told Levi and Ezee as they left us at my place.

Harper went with them, still acting as driver.

I let Alek carry me up into our apartment. We managed to get shoes and clothes off and he talked me into a shower before we collapsed on the bed, too tired to do more than curl up together. Too tired to talk, and for once I was grateful.

I didn't dream. It was daylight when I awoke, pulled on sweats and a teeshirt, and stumbled out to the sizzling smell of bacon. The clock said it was ten in the morning.

Alek stood in the kitchen room without a stitch of clothing under the apron he was wearing.

"It's good to be alive," I said, settling down at the table and admiring the view.

"Lara called while you were still asleep," he said, dropping bacon onto my plate. "She opened the shop, but she has to be gone by noon. I told her I would wake you before then."

Right. Shop. Business. Normal life.

I ate, put on real clothes, braided my hair after swearing over the tangles in it for a good solid twenty minutes, and headed down to my store.

Harper was there, parked in her spot with her laptop on her lap. She smiled up at me as I walked by.

Lara was behind the counter. It was Monday morning, so there wasn't anyone else in. Mondays were usually dead around the store. I was happy about that.

The window was covered in duct tape and a blue tarp. Very attractive. I sighed.

"Harper said a ghoul did that," Lara said. She sounded far too perky about it. "I missed all the fun."

"Fun, right." I looked at her like she was crazy.

"I called the contractor. He said he still has the specs for it and can get a replacement out by Wednesday,"

Lara continued, undaunted by my critical gaze.

"Careful, or Jade will make you employee of the month," Harper said.

I turned my glare on her and found her equally unimpressed.

"I'm already employee of the month," Lara said as she shouldered her backpack.

"You're the only employee," I said.

"Exactly," she said with a grin. "I'll see you both tomorrow. Glad you are alive and all, by the way."

She left the store. When the tinkling of the bells hanging on the door quieted, Harper set aside her laptop and came over to where I stood.

"Thank you," she said, her green eyes searching my face.

I didn't know what she was hoping to see.

"For what?"

"Trusting us to help you," she said with a shrug.

I put my hands on her shoulders as something in my chest tightened and twisted.

"I'm trying," I said.

Harper wrapped her arms around me, yanking me into a hug I gladly returned.

"It's good to be home," she said into my shoulder.

"Sorry about the zombies," I said, chuckling.

"There are worse things in the world," she said. Her tone made me push her back so I could see her face.

"What happened to you while you were gone?" I asked her.

She shrugged again, the movement deliberately casual. Her gaze was hard to meet. There was so much sadness in it that my heart started to break again.

"I can try to tell you about it," she said. "But not today, okay? I get it though. How you tried to run from evil all those years, but it just kept coming anyway."

"Yeah," I said. I wouldn't push her if she wasn't ready to talk. "Evil does that."

"Want to see a cool new trick I learned with Disruptors?" she said, breaking the tense air between us.

"You're playing Protoss?" I said, shocked.

"Practicing off-race, just for variety. Don't worry, my heart is pure Zerg." Harper grinned.

I let her change the subject and went happily to get my nerd on with my best friend. She was right. It was good to be home.

Junebug called and had some choice words for me, but the conversation ended with us chuckling over what a brat Levi was when he was healing, so that was okay. Ezee called to say he was fine. Everyone was healing but safe. No more zombies. No more Nazis or strange shifters trying to shoot us. My shop would be repaired by end of week. All was turning up roses for the most part.

Late Monday night I lay in bed, tired but unable to sleep. I had touched Samir's heart stone to the Alpha and Omega to make sure it stayed dormant, but I kept rubbing it with my thumb.

"Talk," Alek said, rolling over and pulling me against his chest.

I sighed. He did know me way too well.

"I ate his heart," I said. Saying aloud felt strangely freeing.

"I know," Alek said. "And?"

"I didn't have to. He wasn't a sorcerer. I could have just killed him." I snuggled into Alek's warm chest, breathing in his vanilla and musk scent. My D20 was still clutched in my hand, my thumb on the heartstone.

"But you did," Alek said, his voice a rumble in his chest, vibrating slightly against my cheek.

"I don't trust the Archivist," I said. "I know he helped me before, but who knows what his real motivation for that was about? There's so much I don't know. About vampires. About magic. I hope I never have to use the knowledge, but it is better to have and not need than be killed later cause I was unprepared, right?"

"Yes," Alek said. He made it sound so simple.

"Damnit," I muttered. Then I voiced my true fear, something I had trouble sharing even with Alek.

"What if this is how it starts?" I asked. The words I wanted stuck in my throat.

"How it starts?" he repeated.

"What if Samir justified himself the same way in the beginning?" I wasn't sure if he had or not. His journals had gone all the way back, but I hadn't read them all. The entries I had read were full of him talking about what he could get, how strong the victim was, the purpose and range of their magic. More like someone reviewing and describing a meal they'd just consumed than killing a person. "What if I'm sliding down that slope and I don't even realize it?"

"Samir would have eaten Samir," Alek said. His arms tightened around me.

Well, fuck. I couldn't argue with that logic. I wasn't Samir. Not yet. Not ever, if I had any say in it. Which I did, I realized. I had eaten the necromancer's heart, but not without reluctance, without second-guessing myself and my motives. Perhaps the road to hell would be paved with my good intentions, but I wasn't there yet.

"Good talk," I said. I licked his skin and felt him shiver.

"Less talk now," Alek said, rolling me under him.

We were alive. I didn't owe the Archivist a favor anymore. Samir was still a trapped bead of mostly dead. Life was as good as it was going to get for the moment.

Less talk was better.

If you want to be notified when Annie Bellet's next novel or collection is released, please sign up for the mailing list by going to: http://tinyurl.com/anniebellet Your email address will never be shared and you can unsubscribe at any time. Want to find more Twenty-Sided Sorceress books? Go here:
http://overactive.wordpress.com/twenty-sided-sorceress/ for links and more information.

Word-of-mouth and reviews are vital for any author to succeed. If you enjoyed the book, please tell your friends and consider leaving a review wherever you purchased it. Even a few lines sharing your thoughts on this story would be extremely helpful for other readers. Thank you!

Look for *Tribes: Harper's Tale*, the exciting story of Harper's time away from Wylde.

Coming April 2017.

Jade & friends will return in *River of No Return:* Book 9 *of The Twenty-Sided Sorceress*.

Coming Summer 2017.

Also by Annie Bellet

The Gryphonpike Chronicles:
Witch Hunt
Twice Drowned Dragon
A Stone's Throw
Dead of Knight
The Barrows (Omnibus Vol.1)
Brood Mother (Spring 2017)

Chwedl Duology:
A Heart in Sun and Shadow
The Raven King (Winter 2017)

Pyrrh Considerable Crimes Division Series:
Avarice
Wrath (Fall 2017)

Short Story Collections:
Till Human Voices Wake Us
Dusk and Shiver
Forgotten Tigers and Other Stories

About the Author:

Annie Bellet lives and writes in the Pacific NW. She is the *USA Today* bestselling author of the *Gryphonpike Chronicles* and the *Twenty-Sided Sorceress* series. Follow her at her website at www.anniebellet.com

Made in the USA
Columbia, SC
01 September 2019